The Riverview Series
A Novella

A River Between Us

JoAnna Grace

JoAnna Grace

CONTEMPORARY ROMANCES
The Roles We Play

Riverview Romances
Why The River Runs

PARANORMAL TITLES

Divine Chronicle Series:
Divine Awakening
Divine Destiny
Divine Judgment
Divine Encounter
Divine Pursuit

Blake Pride Series:
Pride Before The Fall
Break Her Fall
The Harder They Fall
Divided We Fall

For more information on JoAnna's books, signings, events,
and more,
Sign up for the NEWSLETTER!

A Division of Y&R Enterprises, LLC
PO Box 2283
Lindale, TX 75771

This book is a work of fiction. Therefore, all names, places, characters, and situations are a product of the author's imagination and used fictitiously. Any resemblance to actual persons, living or dead, places, or events is entirely coincidental.

Copyright © 2019 by JoAnna Grace

All rights reserved. No part of this book may be used or reproduced in any manner whatsoever. For information address Y&R Ent. LLC/Arrow Book Works, PO Box 2283, Lindale, TX 75771.

For information about special discounts for bulk purchases, please contact Y&R Ent. LLC/ Arrow Book Works by email at: arrowbkw@gmail.com

Cover Design by Inkstain Design Studio
Book design by Champagne Book Design
Printed in the United States of America

Library of Congress Control Number Data
Grace, JoAnna.
     A River Between Us / JoAnna Grace.
     Fiction. | BISAC: FICTION / Romance / Contemporary. | FICTION / Romance / General. | FICTION / Romance / Short Stories.
LOC # : 201990203
ISBN 978-1-940460-71-0

authorjoannagrace.com
Receive updates from JoAnna

A Note From Jo

Thank you, dear readers, for once again picking up a
JoAnna Grace novel.
I hope you enjoy it.
It brings me great joy to hear from you. Please connect
with me on social media:

Facebook: facebook.com/joannagraceauthor
Twitter: twitter.com/joannagrace4ya
Instagram: instagram.com/authorjoannagrace

Want updates delivered to your inbox? Make sure you're
in the know.
Sign up for my newsletter today!

Do you want to help an author?
Leave a review!
Your opinion matters. Every review can help.

Share a link to this book on social media!
Tag Jo and share this book with your friends.

Support Indie Authors!

Did you know that an Indie Author fronts all the cost of production?

That's right. We appreciate every person who purchases our books because that's how we continue to produce more.

Independent authors, cover designers, editors, and formatters work hard to bring readers quality products and stories they can fall in love with.

Like. Share. Follow. Subscribe. Tag. Review.
It all helps the Indie community!

Share the Love.

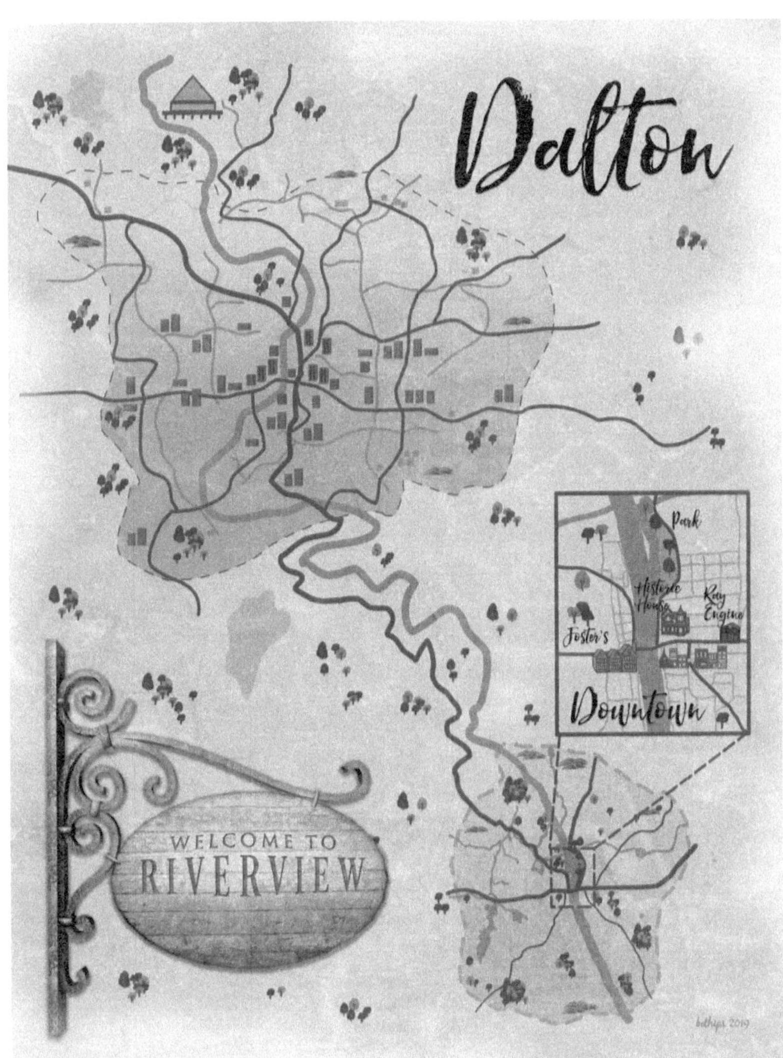

Dalton
Park
Historic House
Ray Engine
Foster's
Downtown
WELCOME TO RIVERVIEW
bethups 2019

Four years ago, down by the river.

Holly's stomach turned cartwheels as she faced Justin Meyers and held his hands.

The minister cleared his throat and smiled. "Repeat after me. I, Holly Grace Combs…"

"I, Holly Grace Combs…" Thank God he said her name. She might've forgotten it, as nervous as she was.

"Take you, Justin Alexander Meyers…"

"Take you, Justin Alexander Meyers…"

"As my lawfully wedded husband."

Husband. Holy hell. Justin would be her husband; to have and to hold until death they did part. She said the words, meant them with all her heart. Justin had been the great love of her life since they were kids playing house together. College had pulled them apart the last couple years, but as he repeated his vows back to her, she knew this was the right thing to do.

The Sanguine River flowed behind them as the preacher pronounced them man and wife and Holly kissed her best friend since childhood in the presence of her brother and his flavor of the week.

"Now, y'all don't get me wrong," said the preacher with a wide smile that shined as bright as the moon on the river. "I don't mind performin' this ceremony 'cause I've known it was comin' since you was both runnin' 'round the playground at church. But y'all might wanna tell your parents b'fore you file the actual paperwork. I usually don't do this without the license. But you got your witnesses present and it's better than you kids livin' in sin, I guess. You're married in God's eyes; that's what counts." He slapped Justin on the back and left with Hunter and his girlfriend.

Holly and Justin stayed hand-in-hand, staring at each other with matching grins, the water flowing gently behind them. She loved his smile. She loved that special spark in his eyes when he smiled at her. No one else saw it. Only Holly.

"We're married," he whispered.

"Yeah, seems that way." Holly met his dark hazel eyes and bit her bottom lip.

Justin ran his fingers over her cheek and through her hair. "I love you, Honeycomb. Always have, always will."

"I love you too." His hand cupped her cheek and she kissed his palm. "Our parents are going to freak out."

"I'm not worried about it."

She let out a huff of air. "You never worry about anything." Which was why she worried about everything.

They laughed and kissed until excitement turned into desire. Justin rented a hotel room down the river and they didn't come up for air until the next afternoon.

Holly lay naked in the bed, her legs intertwined with Justin's. "We have to get back to reality."

Justin propped his head up on his elbow and frowned. "Yeah. We should tell our parents, and our friends…and you should make sure Lance isn't going to be an issue."

Chills vanquished all the elation from the last twenty-four hours. It was time to face her ex-boyfriend once and for all.

Today...

HOLLY SIGHED AND GLANCED AT HER WATCH ONE more time. Only ten minutes had passed since the last time she'd checked it. *Dang.* Twenty more minutes until the bank closed. Those twenty minutes would be busy with everyone trying to deposit or cash their paychecks for the week.

Three and a half years was a long time to work this job. It had quickly become stale. She often found her mind drifting as she sat, waiting for cars to come through. Her thoughts centered on a watery grave that could've been her own, a night that forced her from her hometown and transformed her identity.

Luckily, this Friday afternoon, the line was bustling with cars and her thoughts couldn't go too deep.

She smiled at the customers in the drive-through,

laughed at their poor jokes, and was vigilant about making sure she didn't screw something up. People tended to get upset when you deposited their checks in someone else's accounts or transposed numbers. She had only done that once, when she first started. The screaming woman chewed her a new one right in front of her manager. Thankfully, he was a God-fearing man who believed in second chances.

The bank-teller gig provided her a paycheck, but it wasn't anything her heart was into. She wanted to get home to finish working on the sweet car in her garage. The black 1970 Plymouth Barracuda was her dream come true. An older man who frequented the bank saw her wall calendar and asked if she liked muscle cars or if her boyfriend had given her a crappy birthday gift. Luckily, the drive-through was empty and they talked muscle cars for ten minutes before he told her about his collection. Holly's face must've lit up like Christmas morning, because the man and his wife invited her over for dinner.

The Barracuda had belonged to their son, who was killed many years ago. The wife struggled to let it go until she saw how Holly drooled when her husband removed the tarp. They had to talk it over first, but they finally agreed to sell it cheap to Holly if she swore to fix it up and give it an adventurous life. That vow was the easiest she'd ever made…well, second easiest.

With so much time on her hands, it presented the perfect project. As much as she wanted to call the best mechanic in three counties and tell him all about it, she wouldn't bring herself to dial those numbers.

Holly's direct line rang and she jumped.

"First Bank of Dalton, this is Holly. Can I help you?"

"Holly, good afternoon, this is Danny over here at the

Dalton Monthly Magazine. Um, it's that time again and I know you said last year was your last year, but, uh, all the boys at the fire station were hoping you'd model again for their feature issue."

Her eyes clenched tight and her face drew up. "Isn't it a bit early for that?" Holly still took a light sweater to work during those cool March mornings and the magazine usually didn't feature the firemen until September or October.

"This year, we're doing their feature early."

"Oh…well…I haven't really done any modeling work in a while, Danny. I haven't seen a gym in three months." Her snug dress slacks could testify to that.

Danny had a deep southern drawl to make any woman melt. The voice lent to the image of a tall strapping cowboy who worked shirtless with horses and tilted his hat to women. The reality was *so* not that. "Oh, now, you know that's no deal breaker, Holly. You're still the prettiest girl in Texas and those past issues sold out in a matter of days." He chuckled, and she imagined his face red with blush. "It's a huge fund raiser for the department too."

"In the last three years I've been modeling for this magazine, I've had fifteen marriage proposals, nine men who openly told the bank they would move their accounts here if I personally saw to their *business*, two of which were married, and one full-on stalker whose picture is on the board in the break room as a security risk. I nearly lost my job over that one."

The other woman working the drive-through with her clapped a hand over her mouth to contain her giggle. She had worked with Holly for the last year and knew all the gossip.

Danny guffawed. "Guess it's a handy thing you haven't

been working out, huh? Maybe men won't go crazy this year. The theme is May, men, & muscle cars, and I know you're into that."

She fisted her hand. This was a prime opportunity to show off her new baby. "Can I be in a racing suit instead of a bikini? Maybe even a helmet?"

An indignant snort came from beside her and Holly shushed the other teller.

Danny snickered. "Ah, shucks, Holly, you're centerfold material and you know it. Is that a yes I'm hearing?"

"Danny, if I get another stalker, I swear I'm going to gain fifty pounds and shave my head, ensuring you won't ever ask me again. Got it?"

There was deep, victorious laughter on the other end of the line. "You'd still be the prettiest bald chick in Texas. I sure appreciate you, Holly."

"Don't say that yet. I have two stipulations."

"Uh, sure thing." The hesitation in his voice made her think otherwise.

As she ended the call, her coworker had a single black brow raised on her ebony forehead. "It's a good thing you's pretty. Cause you's a glutton for punishment, sister."

Holly's shoulders slumped and she exhaled a heavy breath.

Two weeks later, when Holly arrived at the outdoor photo shoot, there were at least ten off-duty firemen there. She hopped out of her truck, closed the door, and folded her arms, glaring at Danny, who trotted over. "I only asked for two things, Danny. We use my car, and no guys at the shoot." She ticked off the points with her fingers.

"I'm sorry, really, but if it makes you feel better, they wanted to help with the car. You said it didn't run, right?"

He feigned innocence, raising his hands in surrender.

"Help with the car, my ass."

"Well, they'd help with that too," Danny muttered as Holly rolled her eyes. Even though she was only five foot three inches, Danny met her nose-to-nose. He was a short, thin, slow-speaking bundle of sweetness who handled a lot of the promotions and fund raisers for the fire department. "I hired the same photographer from last year. You liked her, right?"

She sighed, nodding. "At least there's that." As someone who worked as a model all through college, that said something. Holly worked with some of the best photographers in Texas. She forced a smile. "She's great."

The firemen helped her offload the Barracuda from the trailer and push it over to the area the photographer had chosen. All the while, they oohed and ahhed over her baby. A couple volunteered to polish up the car while she changed and did hair and makeup. They were all being civil and polite, but when Holly stepped out of the changing tent in her thin robe and high heels, their attention came straight to her.

This is why I didn't want to do this again.

She walked over to the car, sitting on the bank of the Sanguine River, a perfect sunset in the background. The 'Cuda shined up nicely, she had to admit.

The photographer, Lisa, went right to work, and Holly slipped off the robe, revealing her red bikini and lots of spray-tanned skin. She took a deep breath and wished like hell she hadn't let her gym membership go as she tossed it to the photographer. All the guys went quiet, their eyes wide and round, their tongues hanging out. Danny had apparently told the guys not to say a word, but they were all casually standing around, staring, and ogling her in obvious appreciation.

Being the professional model that she was, Holly tried to focus on the job. Lisa had many connections around Dalton and could refer her to other jobs. Thanks to those connections, Lisa had landed Holly a sweet gig modeling wedding dresses for a local shop's brochures. No matter how much she didn't want to be half naked in the cold air, it was a paying job.

Holly lay on the hood, arched her back, and gave the camera her signature smile, then her smoldering, sexy stare. Each pose loosened her up and, eventually, the guys didn't stay silent any longer. The jokes and innuendoes started and Holly giggled. *Men.*

"That's the sexiest…uh…*hood* I've ever seen."

"Holly, he wants under your hood."

She smirked and walked to the front of the car, opened the hood, and bent over the bumper, casting a deliberately sexy wink his way, the photographer capturing it all. The tall, handsome fireman grasped his heart dramatically, entertaining his buddies. The environment of the shoot lightened and it was a positive reminder of why she did the calendar in the first place.

These guys worked hard, gave their time, and risked their lives for the community. It took bravery and honor to do that. Their calendar fundraiser helped get these men the equipment and training needed to keep people safe. If putting on a bikini helped that way, why not? Thanks to the good Lord and good genes, her physical attributes were blessed.

"Let's get a group shot," Lisa said, waving the guys over to the car at the end of the shoot. Some of them jumped at the opportunity, while some of them were more shy. The one guy of the group who was openly smitten with her came jogging over. The photographer put him right in front of the car, leaning on the windshield. The other guys were positioned around the car and, being men, had some of their own suggestions.

"Should we pretend that we're washing it?"

"I vote for a wet t-shirt contest."

"We should mimic Holly's poses," one guy said as he opened the hood and stuck his butt out, then fluttered his lashes at the camera.

"Oh, yes!" Holly teased. "Work it, work it, baby."

A couple of the other *sillier* men copied her poses as the more stoic guys filled in the gap. Lisa gave Holly one of her extra cameras and told her to get in the picture.

"Jump up there, piggy-back on that tall one," the photographer said.

"Oh yeah." The fireman nodded and held out his arms. "Come on, cutie-pie. I've gotcha."

Internally cringing, Holly hopped up and wrapped her arms around his neck. She was all too aware of his hands on her bare thighs, holding her up.

"That's the cover, right there." Lisa snapped a ton of pictures and Danny nodded his head.

After the shoot was over, the car loaded, and Holly was in full clothing again, she hoped herself free and clear of the men. She exchanged goodbyes with Lisa, thanking her for a fun day and reminding her to keep Holly in mind for future projects. She collected a check from Danny and thought about all the things she could fix on the 'Cuda with the money. Only steps away from her truck, she heard the cute one call her name. He came jogging over, a huge, gorgeous smile on his face.

He's so hot. A wave of guilt hit her.

"Hey, cutie-pie!"

Lord, but he was tall and built, nice smile, nice eyes. Practically perfect. He could've been in that photoshoot with her. They could grace the covers of romance novels worldwide. Her stomach cramped up, nervous that she might possibly be attracted to him.

"Hi." She pushed her hair behind her ears and pasted on a kind grin.

He held out a hand. "I'm Ben."

Being raised a true southern girl, she gave a firm handshake. "Holly. Nice to meet you, Ben." Holly had never been rude to a person in her life. She wasn't going to start now. That was not how Mama raised her.

"Thanks for doing all this. Danny said the last few years have been a real success." Ben twisted his hands together. His massive shoulders swayed as he rocked from foot to foot.

Was he nervous?

"So he says. I don't believe him, but I'm happy to help." Holly played with her keys.

"Your car is great." He stepped towards the trailer holding the 'Cuda. "Your boyfriend's?"

Yep, he went there.

Heat rose in her neck and made its way up to her cheeks. "Mine. No boyfriend. That was a smooth way of asking, though. Good job."

Ben smiled and shrugged innocently. "Can't blame a guy for trying, right?"

"I guess not." Holly wanted to melt at his smile. How many women had fallen into his blue eyes and got lost in the desire found there? Thanks to her past, she always wondered what was behind charming smiles.

"Who's rebuilding it for you?"

Truth or a lie? Truth or a lie? Damn you, morals. "I'm, um, doing it myself."

At this point, she usually received one of two reactions. One, they balked and didn't believe that a model also worked with her hands, much less could be a mechanic. Because somehow it fried the man's brain that a pretty girl might be anything more than pretty. Or two, they practically started drooling and went retarded, acted like they'd found the holy grail of women. *Which way you going, Ben?*

His brows raised high. "No kidding? That's, wow, that's cool." He tilted his head, "Danny said you worked at a bank?"

"I do. This is a hobby. The day job pays for parts."

Ben nodded and ran a hand through his dark-blonde hair. "You're full of surprises, Holly." He took a deep breath and met her eyes. "Wow, you've left me no choice. I'm going to have to ask you out now."

Holly chuckled, genuinely entertained. "Oh, you *have* to?"

Dimples formed on his cheeks. "It's your fault, truly. There's no other direction to go from here. We have to talk cars over dinner."

As charming as he was, Holly feared relationships more than anything. She possessed more complications and baggage than most men possessed patience to handle. Holly's mouth opened to kindly reject his offer, but her phone chimed with an incoming text.

Tina is getting married. OMG! Get your ass home so we can celebrate.

Jayden's message hit her in the gut. As excited as she was for one of her best friends, it only reminded her of how far away she was from her dream life. Married. Kids. Happy. She had been so close with Justin, but fate had not been kind to them.

"Everything okay?" Ben asked, his voice kind.

"One of my best friends is getting married."

Ben narrowed his eyes at her. "That's exciting, right? Why do you look so sad?"

Holly shook her head and smiled. "Oh, no, I'm thrilled for her. It's great news; surprising, but great. What were you saying?"

"I'd love to take you out. Maybe dinner…tonight?" Ben's blue eyes begged her to say yes.

Life was moving on in Riverview without her. Of all their friends, Tina was the last person anyone expected to settle down and get married, yet here she was, taking a huge step in her life. Of all their friends, no one wanted to be married and have a family as much as Holly. Meg had run off to Boston and gotten married, had a baby. Jayden was already a widow, Keri and Marshall were going strong. Even her brother had a steady girlfriend.

If she didn't get her ass in gear, she might as well start collecting cats, mu-mus, and calling everyone Moon-pie.

"Dinner sounds great." Holly returned the huge smile that Ben flashed her.

At some point, Holly had to be brave or she was never going to move on with her life.

"**Y**OU WENT ON A *WHAT*?" TINA FOSTER SCREECHED on the other end of the phone line as they talked a few days later. "Do you even remember what a date is? Do I need to explain it to you to make sure you're not hallucinating?" Her laughter coaxed a smile from Holly.

"Yes, smartass. I know what a date is."

"And you went on one? With a man? A *real* one, not one of those blow-up things or something battery-operated?"

Holly chuckled. "Kiss my ass, T. He's a hot firefighter named Ben. We met on a photo shoot I did for the magazine. And we've had two dates, not one. Thank you very much."

"Two?" Tina whistled a descending note. "I'm really proud of you, Honey. That's a monumental step."

"Not really. Just a natural one." Holly tried to take a page out of Tina's book and think logically.

"Great. So that means you have a plus one for the wedding?"

"Hold your horses, cowgirl. It's barely spring time. You're not getting married until what, Christmas? Let's not get crazy, T. We had a couple dates, that's all." Holly fell onto the couch in her cabin and gazed out the two-story A-frame windows out to the calm waters of the Sanguine. She wanted to be thrilled for Tina, but the emotion was only surface level. Deep down, she was sick to her stomach at the idea of being forced to go back to Riverview.

People were cheerful at weddings. People laughed and smiled and took pictures. They reunited with loved ones they haven't seen in ages. That sent chills over her skin. What if people found out why she'd left town? What if they started asking what happened to her own marriage?

Not allowing herself to go there, she focused on Tina's wedding. "Has Bo chosen his groomsmen yet?"

She didn't have to ask who Tina's bridesmaids were. Jayden, the obligatory cousin or two, Keri, and, hopefully, her. If Meg's controlling husband gave her the money for a plane ticket, maybe Meg. Their other friend, Lynette, was off on safari or walk-about or something crazy on another continent. Who knew if she'd show up?

"You'll never believe this." Tina's voice lowered and Holly imagined her crouching over the phone to whisper. "Do you remember Andrew Buchanan?"

Yeah, she did. Super-hot, super mysterious, super-talented guy. "The spy or assassin or whatever rumors people came up with?"

"Yeah. Turns out, he's the only guy who kept up with Bo while he was, uh, on his forced vacation." That was their polite way of saying "incarceration." "He's on some assignment in Europe, but he's trying to come back home to take care of his dad and be in the wedding."

"You're going to have 007 in your wedding party? That's cool."

The girls chuckled. "Right! The best man will be packing, that's for sure. Other than him, Bo only has two friends in town. Jason, the guy on my crew, is standing for him. Bear is there more for me than Bo, and Marshall said he would walk with his wife if we needed someone to even it up."

"Who's the other friend?"

"Huh?" Tina's voice rose an octave.

Holly chuckled. Sometimes even Tina had blonde moments. "You said he has two friends in town. Bear and Marshall were more for you, so it's Jason and who? Do I know him?" Holly kicked off her heels and rubbed her feet.

"Uh, well, you know that old truck of Bo's breaks down all the time and so he's always having to work on it. It was his grandfather's and I know it means a lot to him, but seriously, he should let it go, you know? It's falling apart and—"

"You're rambling." Holly took a deep breath.

Tina went quiet. "It's Justin."

Holly sat up straight on the couch, her feet falling to the floor with a thud. "What?"

"They're friends, Holly." Tina spoke softly, as if to a child. "They've spent a lot of time working in his truck together. Justin has been a positive influence for him too. They hang out a lot."

"Damn it, Tina."

Tina immediately got defensive. "What? They hit it off—"

"Of all the mechanics in town, you *had* to send your

boyfriend to Justin, did you?"

Tina growled on the other end of the phone. "Of *course* I sent him to Justin. He's the best. And Bo wasn't my boyfriend at the time. How was I to know they would become buds? Why should I avoid one of my childhood friends because you chose to stick your head in the sand?"

Here they were, back to their old argument, the one thing Holly and Tina fought about. "I'm not sticking my head in the sand. I'm moving on."

"No, you're avoiding, you're distracting, you're suppressing. But you're not moving on. You can't move on without dealing with the past and—"

"It's not that simple and you know it." Holly groaned. "Not everyone is like you, Tina. We can't all nail people's clothes to their desk and call it closure. I'm happy for you, Tina, I am. I hope you know that. But maybe I'm not the right person to be in your bridal party."

Tina gasped. "Holly, no, come on—"

"I'm sorry. I have to go." Holly ended the call and threw her phone on the couch, but Tina immediately called her back. She walked out onto the back porch and put a closed door between her and the ringing cell phone. It took twenty minutes to calm her heart rate. She sat on the edge of the pier and dipped her feet in the river water. It still held the bite of the winter.

Nights like this made her thankful for her little piece of heaven on the Sanguine River, far from Riverview. The cabin sat tucked in the woods among huge live oak trees. This part of the river, north of Dalton, narrowed too much for all the boat traffic and the typical water activities, but it was quite deep.

Over the last four years, she'd learned the cycles of the

water. The river had a life that carried on despite what the rest of the world did, and she appreciated that. If Mother Nature felt generous, the river ran swift and hard, carving out more of the banks. She didn't swim during those seasons; the current would take her all the way to town. There weren't too many surprises with this river. No flash floods, no disastrous currents that damaged homes or piers. Holly loved the river's consistency and steadfastness.

If only it were that simple with life.

For years, she worked to keep her life simple, free of drama, upset, or shock; everything that Riverview embodied. Life in Dalton had balance, a rhythm that kept her demons at bay and the ghosts in the closet. If she wasn't at the bank, she worked on the car. If she ran out of money to work on the car, she painted or sketched, anything to keep her mind busy. She was one of a hundred thousand people going about their routines in Dalton. One more pretty face in the crowd, one more nobody working her day job.

Not in Riverview. There, she was something else, something different, something darker.

It wasn't always like that. Before that September night years ago, she had been naive and carefree. Nothing could touch her. She spent her college years in Carreyville, by the coast, studying art and photography, breezing through while she and Hunter did small-time modeling and lived it up. They both dated and partied, but nothing too extreme. Their agent would skin them alive otherwise.

While she was in college, the relationship with Justin was put on hold. He became preoccupied with going to the car races and, for a while, worked on a pit crew until his step-father needed help back in Riverview. The weekends she came home, they were attached at the hip. When he touched her, the world spun fast, the stars aligned, and everything was perfect.

It wasn't until her last semester that Lance Smith, Meg's brother, showed up in Carreyville along with Sean Harris and a couple other guys. They rented a house together on the beach for the summer. Hunter and Holly naturally hung out with them and spent a lot of time there.

Lance Smith was one of the most popular guys in Riverview and that charisma made him just as popular with the college kids in Carreyville. He knew how to party, how to entertain. He was her best friend's older brother, a sexy, fun, fiery redhead. That magnetic personality made him seem larger than life. The man had a way with jokes, telling stories that left people in stitches, and captivating anyone he spoke to.

That was how he snagged her. Holly was a model and Lance's tastes required the best of everything. He had to have her, pursued her relentlessly, used Meg to get insight to what she liked.

Despite what her heart told her, she'd given in and started dating Lance during one of the many breaks she and Justin took. It went well for a while, a perfect match from the outside. It took a few months before things went south. No one realized a thing was wrong. Holly kept up the charade in fear of what the truth would do to Meg, who adored Lance and was already calling Holly her sister-in-law. If she found out what a monster her brother was—

A plastic bottle of oil fell off the shelf in her storage area and scared her right out of her thoughts and her skin.

What the hell?

She stood and slowly peeked around the corner of her house to the lean-to where she kept her supplies. There was nothing there, but she couldn't shake the feeling of being watched. Her heart sped up and she swallowed. *Paranoid much?* Living alone in a remote cabin had often inspired her imagination of what might lurk in dark shadows. Fear came easy with Lance Smith on the mind.

She took a deep breath and went to her lounge chair on the back porch. Every day, she lived with the physical and mental scars of their relationship. Each time she stared at the river too long, she could still see the headlights of the car sink beneath the water. Sometimes a swift current in the river scared her so much, she wouldn't swim for weeks, afraid of reliving the night she nearly drowned. Those days of living in fear should be over and she consistently had to remind herself that Lance was gone.

A second later, the fish net fell against the wooden decking and she screamed. Holly jumped up out of her chair, tripped on the leg, and smacked down on the wooden patio, coming face to face with the ugliest damn cat she'd ever seen.

"Ahh!" She scrambled to get to her feet.

The cat didn't move, only watched her clumsiness. The brown in its coat ranged in color from sandy brown to crap brown and patches of the long fur were missing. Poor thing must've lost a hell of a fight with a lawnmower and had the scars to prove it. It hissed at her and bowed its back; even the sound was pathetic.

"What the—where did you come from? Oh my God, you're ugly."

The nearest neighbors had dogs, *big* dogs…maybe that was where this dirty dishrag got so messed up? Either way, it didn't matter; she hated cats and this one had already scared the life out of her.

"Get! Go on." Holly waved her arms and tried to shoo it away, but it simply stared at her as if she was the one invading his space. "Go away, dang it!" Holly used the fishing net to prod it along until the stupid animal thought she was trying to play. It started swatting its paw at the net. "Oh, good grief, stop it. I'm not playing with you, stupid. Go away. Get!"

The mangy cat ran a few feet back and once again hissed.

"Yeah, well, I don't give a rat's furry butt about you either. So find someone else to bother." Holly grumbled all the way to her back door to go inside.

As soon as she cracked the door open, a crap-colored blur darted through her legs and into the house, straight under the couch. "No! No no no. Ugh." Grabbing the broom, she made as much noise and racket as possible. She poked under her couch and tried to piss the cat off enough to run back out the door. No such luck. If the animal was a stray, she didn't want to risk getting scratched or bitten. Who knew what diseases it carried? Getting multiple shots because of this fur ball did not sound appealing at all.

She moved her couch and it remained hidden. She sprayed bug spray under the couch, but then guilt hit her. Just her luck, the stupid thing would die from the chemicals, then she would have a dead cat on her hands. Tuna, milk, her last piece of chocolate. It moved for nothing.

Half an hour later, the cat was still under her couch.

Holly collapsed on the hard wood and let the broom slap down beside her on the floor. A heavy sigh escaped and she leaned her head against the front of her couch. "Fine, you ugly rat bastard, sleep under there. I don't care. Snuggle with the dust bunnies." Her eyes closed, and for a moment, the world was quiet, until her cell phone rang. She reached over her head, grabbing it off the couch from where it landed earlier. It was probably Tina again. Maybe Holly had been too hard on her. She needed to apologize. "Hello?"

"Holly."

In an instant, Holly's heart went from zero to sixty. The air expelled from her lungs and she wouldn't have been more wide awake if doused with ice cold water. Her back went straight as a board and she whispered his name.

"J-Justin."

He cleared his throat. "Tina called." Maybe he paused, expecting a comment, but Holly lost the ability to breathe, much less speak. "I'm not going to be in the wedding. I'm not even going. You can be there for Tina without having to worry about me, okay?" The words were clipped, hard, and matter-of-fact, not at all the way he spoke to her in the past.

Holly opened her mouth, but the only things that came out were broken sounds. "Uh, um, ah." She clamped her eyes shut and tried to engage her brain. "You're—that's not—you don't—no."

Shit! She slapped a hand over her forehead.

"You've been friends with T since high school and I've only recently reconnected with Bo. If I need to make up some excuse, I can. It's more important for you to be there for her. I'm sorry it has come to this." He let out a heavy sigh and she pictured his head falling backwards the way it did when he was aggravated. Holly knew every nuance about him, every habit, every tick and twitch he made. "You wanted time. I've given you nearly four years. You wanted space. I've stayed away." He huffed and his voice cracked. "You want me to miss my friend's wedding so you can attend without drama, fine. But this is the last straw. I love you, Holly, always have, always will. My life has been on hold long enough, though. I'm done."

There was such resolute sadness in his voice that tears came to her eyes. "You're *done*?"

Right about that time, the bastard cat let out a meow that rivaled nails on a chalkboard or a rusty screen door opening. The screech was so loud that Holly covered her other ear and cursed.

"What the hell was that? Is something dying over there?"

She groaned and wiped her eyes. "It's a cat."

"A *cat* made that noise? A *house* cat or something wild on TV?"

"It's a house cat…I suspect." The mangled cat didn't move from its hideout. "It's protesting under my couch."

"You hate cats." Justin's voice sounded less angry and more skeptical.

"It won't get the hell out of my house." Holly chuckled despite herself. "Stupid rat bastard."

"Me or the cat?" A hint of humor leached into Justin's voice and her stomach fluttered.

Holly sniffed and wiped her nose. "The cat. He looks like crap and more crap mated."

Justin cleared his throat on the other end of the phone. It covered his laugh. "You've always had a way with words."

Holly bit the inside of her cheek, finally engaging her brain. "Don't miss the wedding. Please. If you're one of Bo's friends, he needs you. You should be there. Tina knows everyone in town; she won't miss me."

"Of course she will, Holly. So will everyone else, despite what you assume."

Holly gnawed on her inner cheek and then her nails. "I'll figure it out. Maybe I can show up for the wedding and not all the other stuff. I don't know. Don't bail. Tina and Bo deserve to have their perfect day and that includes you."

"And you."

"And me," she sighed. "It'll be fine."

Justin let out another loud breath on the other end of the line. "Okay, Honey. You need me to call T?"

"I owe her an apology. I'll call her." Holly put her head between her legs. She was going to be sick.

"You're right to move on with your life, Holly. I guess it's time for me to start moving on with mine too. We've drug this thing out far too long. I'll have the divorce papers mailed to you."

Oh God! "Justi—"

"Bye, Honey." *Click.*

Holly threw her cell phone against the wall and raked her hands through her hair. *Divorce papers.* She hadn't even thought about the paperwork; they had been separated for so long. Guilt rolled like angry waves in her gut. She'd gone on dates with Ben and not thought twice about it. There was no way Justin had been single all this time. She figured he had moved on too. Had he been faithful? Four years was a long time for a social guy like him to be alone. *Surely not.* Then again, Justin was the best man she knew.

Memories flooded her mind as she made herself a stiff drink and tried to relax.

He had been the embodiment of her dreams all through her teenage years. Back then, he was wild and crazy, constantly going to car races on the weekends and working on racecars for various drivers. It was his obsession. All his focus was on the track and working on a pit crew.

After she and Hunter moved south to Carreyville for college and modeling jobs, Justin hadn't been able to adjust to the long-distance relationship. He was an exceptionally physical person, needing the connection from holding hands or kissing or simply curling up on the couch together. The distance took its toll and they put things on hold to pursue their different careers, knowing they would always find their way back to each other.

Then along came Lance.

When they were together, it was a party. Lance was intense, so lively and full of laughter and desire. He bragged about how he had the prettiest girl in Texas, how much he loved Holly, and how they were going to be together forever. In the many months they dated, however, he never once moved to propose, or showed that he intended to make good on his word when they were alone. After a while, a girl had to wonder if it wasn't all for show.

The problem began when he would call during class, wanting to know exactly where she was, who she was with, and what she was doing. He never believed her. She could be innocently studying with her girlfriends and he would call, wanting to know what guys were there and accuse her of cheating. The paranoia slowly grew worse. He would track her cell phone, call her brother, call her roommate, whatever it took to locate her. A couple times, he showed up outside her classes and would pick a fight with whoever she talked with as she exited the room.

Lance drove the final nail in the coffin when he missed her college graduation. On the weekend she wanted to be surrounded with those she loved, he disappeared with Sean Harris to a concert two states away and hadn't told her a thing. Sean had already started his descent into drugs and would sleep with anyone. Holly had asked several times for Lance to not hang out with Sean, but there he was, hundreds of miles away, at a rock concert, high or drunk or both, judging by his slurred words. After a fuming phone call, she realized their relationship was going nowhere. He didn't respect her, he didn't care about her feelings, and, no matter how he professed it in public, Lance damn sure hadn't been in love with her.

Instead, she packed up her things after graduation and went home, back to Riverview, back to her family.

Back then, Chris and Jayden Harris were hosting one of their famous cookouts and Jayden begged her to come visit, celebrate her graduation, and say hello to everyone. Holly showed up and ran right into Justin.

"Honey!" He picked her up in his strong arms and twirled her around. "Man, you're more beautiful than ever." His eyes sparkled when they met hers, sending her heart racing in her chest. "I didn't know you were home."

"Yeah, for the foreseeable future. Graduated with a degree in art. Don't know what I'll do with it, but I have it. Lance is off with Sean doing God only knows what…or who." She bounced from one foot to another, nervous and giddy to see him.

Justin's face fell. "Y'all are still together, huh? I didn't expect that."

"Yeah, I guess." Having to admit that to Justin, the one guy she'd always been crazy about, was harder than she realized. "But I'm done. He's not a stable, um, he's not…*you*." There was an awkward pause as their eyes met and sparks flew. "I need a drink."

"You look like I need a drink too." Justin found her a wine cooler, then another, and another. They sat on the tailgate of his truck, in the middle of the Harris's pasture, watching the bonfire and listening to the radio for hours. When everyone else left, Justin and Holly stayed. They laughed and talked and flirted until the bonfire died and the sun came up.

Jayden found them the next morning, wrapped up in a blanket against the chilly March morning air. Nothing had happened that night, but it reignited the flames between them. She had to deal with Lance when he returned. Until then, she and Justin were attached at the hip, same as when they were teenagers. They spoke each other's language. No matter how much time passed between them, they always picked right back up, being best friends and being in love.

Not long after, he had taken her down by the river and promised to love her forever.

Holly held those memories close as she prepared for bed that night, wiping away her tears. Now, four years later, they were about to sign divorce papers. Justin was talking about moving on and perhaps it was time, no matter how much it broke her heart.

She stared at her reflection. *Time to let him go…even if it rips me in two.*

Justin Meyers wiped the transmission fluid off his hands with his dirty rag. *Might be time to get a clean one.* There was only so much dirt one could wash off with dirt. His mind kept replaying the sound of Holly's voice last night. It sounded sadder than he remembered, so devoid of happiness and joy. It was hollow at best.

What happened to her?

Everyone felt terrible after Lance's death. It was a tragedy, for sure. But why did Holly determine it was her fault that his car hydroplaned? She had taken the blame for that since day one. As if she had the power to control a drunk guy behind the wheel. No matter how many times he tried to comfort her, she'd always said it was her fault. *I don't get it.*

Before Lance *effing* Smith came into the picture, he and Holly never had secrets between them. He knew her like the back of his hand and she knew him just as well. Now they had so many unsaid words, so many secrets, and so many miles of the Sanguine River between them, that he often wondered if the same waters flowed by them both.

Despite it all, he had never stopped loving her, never stopped wishing he could be her husband in more than just a legal sense.

"What up, grease monkey?" Hunter Combs, Holly's twin and one of his best friends, sauntered in to Ray's Engine.

"Not much, pretty boy. You?" They shook hands and grinned at their nicknames for each other that had lasted since high school.

Hunter Combs was a disgustingly well-put-together dude, his face so identical to his sister's, it made Justin's chest hurt. Hunter had the same striking blue eyes, perfect teeth, prominent cheekbones, and impeccable style as Holly. It was the hair that differentiated the twins. Hunter had dirty-blonde hair, bordering on light brown. Holly's hair was a light, striking honey. Which was how she earned her nickname, Honeycomb. She never liked it, said it was too cheesy. Most people just called her Honey. Both Combs twins were model quality and had cashed in on their pretty faces.

"I'm all right. Can't complain." Hunter grinned. He never complained. "You have time for lunch?"

"Always have time for food. Don't know if I want to go anywhere with you." He leaned in and gave Hunter a sniff. "Are you wearing *perfume*?" Justin shook his head and curled his lips in mock disgust.

"It's by Creed, so screw you." Hunter laughed.

Justin scoffed. "The only Creed a man needs to know

about is the boxer, just sayin'."

"Don't hate 'cause I'm on point. Besides, Bear said he would make an exception and only let your dirty ass in the restaurant if I'm with you."

"Bullshit." Justin grabbed his wallet. "What brings you across town? No golf games to play today? No fancy luncheons to attend with your investors?"

Hunter shook his head and shrugged his shoulders. No doubt the pullover he wore had the name of some uppity designer on the label. "Nah, had some land to view west of town. These guys are thinking about opening a manufacturing plant for plastic fittings…or bolts…or some crap. I don't know. I just sell the property."

"Damn, you actually had to work?" Justin slid into Hunter's BMW convertible.

"Suck it and don't ruin my leather, grease monkey." Hunter pulled the sleek sports car onto the street and slid on his Gucci sunglasses. Justin was there when he bought them and choked on the price tag.

Hunter was a cool-headed guy who dressed in designer duds at all times. That pretty face and confident air worked to benefit everything he did.

Justin rarely cared that much. He left the modeling to the model.

They fell into their normal conversations and banter on the way across Riverview to Bear's Bar and Grill.

Jake "Bear" Harris lived up to his name. He was nearly six and a half feet of loud and crazy. Son of a gun ran his restaurant like a boss, though. His new restaurant kept breaking records and winning awards for everything from best food to best atmosphere to best local brew-house. Bear practically lived at the bar and his labor paid off in spades.

He was also one of the most eligible bachelors in Riverview. Not many people realized why he was still single.

The two of them had a lot in common in that area.

"What's up, bro?" Bear bumped their knuckles and flashed one of his broad smiles. He shrugged out of his black BBG jacket and joined them at a table with a hefty sigh. "Man, it feels nice to sit for a minute."

"You've been busy," Hunter said.

"Always, thank God. What're y'all doing today?"

They ordered beers and food from the cute waitress and caught up on what their favorite NFL teams had done in recent games. Bear was a dang football fanatic. He memorized every player on every team, NFC and AFC, and most of their stats. He had opinions on every coach, defensive coordinator, offensive coordinator, owner, manager, and commentator in the game. When in the hell he had time to even watch a game, Justin had no clue. The dude knew his stuff, though.

"Man, can you believe Tina Hard-Ass Foster is getting married?" Hunter shook his head and stuck a chip in his mouth. "Never thought I'd see the day. Bo has some balls hitchin' up to that pony."

"He won't if he ever hurts her," Bear grumbled.

Justin raised a brow. "Jealous much?" Did Bear have a thing for Tina and he missed it?

"Not like that. I mean, yeah, T's my girl, you know? She freaking grew up at my house. She's practically my little sister."

"A little sister who can whip your ass." Hunter chuckled. Bear didn't disagree.

"Bo's good people." Over the last few months, Justin had gotten fairly close to the guy while they turned wrenches and talked shop. "He can handle her."

"Handle her?" Bear blanched and glanced around the restaurant, making sure they didn't get caught. "Don't let her hear you say that crap. She'd nail your damn nuts to one of my tables." They shared a laugh, not at Tina, but at her antics. "For real, I'm happy for 'em. They've literally been through the fire together."

"Hopefully, *someone* around here gets their happily ever after." As soon as the bitter words left his mouth, Justin regretted it. Bear and Hunter gave him matching sympathetic glances before skirting their eyes away.

Bear cleared his throat. "Yeah, well, ya know. People enjoy weddings and come home for stuff like that." He met Justin's eyes and stared expectantly. Hunter did the same.

"What?"

Rolling his eyes, Hunter pushed his plate away. "Have you called my sister yet?"

Justin kept his eyes down and moved the food around his plate with his fork. "We talked last night."

"And?" Hunter prompted him.

"And she's going to be a bridesmaid." *Do we have to freaking talk about this right now?*

"And?" Bear, this time.

Justin put down his fork and tossed his napkin on the table. "And…Tina said she went on an effing date, okay? She's moving on and so will I."

The guys were speechless for a solid minute until Hunter swore under his breath. "Sorry, man. I really hoped she would come around."

"Me too. Oh well."

His friends didn't know about their marriage; only Hunter. It killed them to keep it a secret from their best friends, but given Holly's years of avoidance and denial, it was for the best.

"You're giving up?" Bear's eyes held a similar pain. He, too, pined for a woman who slipped through his fingers. They had an unspoken pact to back each other up when times got hard and they were ready to give up on their loves.

"It's been four years, Bear. Four damn years. How long am I supposed to wait? Tina said she went out with some guy up there in Dalton a couple times. She ain't coming back, not to me anyway."

Filing for an official divorce had written the final chapter in the story of their life-long relationship. He had lost the one epic love of his life and coming to grips with that was going to take a lot of whiskey.

"This doesn't jack with us, right?" Hunter scowled and wiggled his finger between them. "We're still cool?"

Justin rolled his eyes. "Sure, sugar. We'll still braiding each other's hair at sleepovers."

Bear pitched his head back and howled with laughter. Hunter simply flipped him the bird.

"Well, you two bromancers don't forget you're taking me out for my birthday this weekend," Bear reminded them. "For once, I don't want to have to cook or clean up after a party, 'kay?"

"You got it, man." The guys had already made plans to celebrate Bear's twenty-ninth birthday. Their crew of friends were slowly crossing over the thirty-threshold. It struck Justin that at twenty-seven, he had spent all his twenties so far waiting on Holly. First, waiting while she was in college and living in Dalton. Then while she worked through the trauma of nearly dying. He was knocking on the door of thirty and hadn't moved forward in his love life since he was nineteen. It had always been Holly, and, if he was honest with himself, it always would be.

"Hey," Bear rubbed the back of his neck. "You guys mind if Sean tags along?"

"Sean?" Hunter wrinkled his nose. "Does this mean he's doing better?"

Bear shrugged a huge shoulder. "After his failed attempt to jump off the dam, he swears he had some religious experience or something. I don't know. But he put himself into rehab and he's been clean for about seven months now. I don't like the idea, but my mom asked if I'd try to patch things up with him, you know?"

Justin, who had been one of Sean's buddies at one time, nodded his head. "Yeah, man. We can invite him. Glad to hear he's doing well."

Bear nodded. "Thanks. It would be nice to have my brother back, but I'm not holding my breath."

"Hey." Hunter leaned in, his eyes narrowed. "You hear Andrew Buchanan is coming back to town?"

"Yeah. So?" He shoved a fry in his mouth.

"So? Do you believe all that crap about him being some kind of assassin or secret agent for the FBI?"

Justin huffed a laugh, his shoulders popping up. "Why? You going to ask for his autograph?"

"No, jackass." Hunter shook his head and leaned back in his chair. "It's intriguing, though."

"Damn, you gossip like a girl." Justin chuckled.

Bear grinned. "I'm sure he'd like to come to your sleepovers, sugar."

Hunter's face went slack. "You suck. Never mind. Both of you can kiss my ass."

The guys shared a laugh and Justin settled into their

comfortable banter. That evening, he pulled his motorcycle into the garage and dragged his tired ass upstairs to his apartment. It took two rounds of Go-Jo before he cleaned all the grease and oil off his arms and around his fingers.

He heated up a frozen dinner and turned on some races. It didn't matter what or who was racing. If humans rode badass machines and competed to see who came out ahead, he would watch. Hell, he even liked horse races.

On most nights, the television provided a distraction. Not tonight. All he pictured was Holly in some other guy's arms. Her lips, lips he had missed for years, kissing someone else.

Jealousy burned inside and he rubbed his eyes. All these years he waited, and she had the nerve to go on a date with someone else? Justin threw the remote across the room.

There had been plenty of opportunities for him to date. A couple didn't even blanch when he said he was married. But he stayed faithful to his wife, giving her all the time and space a person could want.

Goddamn idiot.

Days later, he still wrestled with the reality of Holly on a date. Instead of wallowing in his sorrows, he reached out to Sean. Maybe mending that relationship wouldn't be in vain.

"Hey, man." Justin gripped his hand as he came into the office of the shop.

"Hey. How's it going?" Sean appeared alert, healthier than he had in many years. His eyes were brighter and he didn't twitch as much.

"Good. Good. You look better."

Sean smiled timidly. "Yeah, I'm good. Real good. I'm

clean and sober."

"Good." Justin didn't know what else to say. *Glad you got your head out of your ass? What the hell was wrong with you? Why did you try to commit suicide?* He stuck with pleasantries. "That's good."

Sean cracked a signature dimpled Harris smile and rocked back on his heels. "So, now that we've established we're both *good*, what did you want to talk to me about?" There was that Harris sense of humor.

Saved. "Right, so the guys are all going out for Bear's birthday this weekend. You in?"

Rocking from one foot to the other, Sean grimaced. "Who's going? I don't reckon I'm welcome in my brother's circles anymore, you know?"

"Bear wants you to come. It's his birthday. It's going to be me, Hunter, Marshall, Bo—"

Sean sucked air through his teeth and shook his head. "Bad idea. I'm pretty sure Bo still thinks I had something to do with the fire."

They had all hoped Sean wasn't one of the people who threw Molotov cocktails at Tina's place and sent it up in flames, nearly killing Tina, her dad, and Bo. In the months since then, they had gotten a confession from the real arsonist. No one considered Sean capable of something so horrible—at least not sober Sean.

"Nah, man. None of us believed that."

"Bear did," Sean said quickly. "He and Tina called me that night, accusing me of helping Rodman set the fire. I didn't, though, I swear."

Justin waved it off. "Heat of the moment, man. They were both scared. They know you didn't do anything; we all do."

"I'll consider it, how 'bout that?" Sean tried to smile. His eyes were much more haunted than Justin remembered. Sean hadn't dealt well with the sudden deaths they had all experienced. First, Lance had died. Sean had been super close to him, especially since they partied together. They all suspected that Lance was the person who got Sean hooked on pot and meth in the first place.

Not two years later, his brother Christopher died and Sean went downhill from there. More drugs, booze, and poor life decisions. He dropped out of trade school and moved in with one of his useless drug buddies.

The fire at Tina's had been some sort of trigger and he attempted suicide off the dam, but that backfired. Whatever happened to him while he was in the hospital was the wakeup call he needed.

Now he needed an invitation to come back to the fold and Justin would happily extend it. "That's enough for me." He clapped hands with Sean and pulled him in for a quick hug, slapping him on the back.

"Hey, um, since I'm here, I'm gonna hit you up about something." Sean glanced around. "My parents are letting me move back into the apartment above the garage, you know, which is great, but I, uh, I need a job. They want rent and utilities, which I'm cool with if it gets me out the rehab shelter. You know anyone who's hiring? I almost made it through trade school, so you know, I can work on things."

Justin and his step-dad had a busy shop, and they always found use for another set of hands to help clean the shop, arrange inventory, pick up parts and things. But he didn't know how Charlie would feel about hiring Sean. "Let me talk to Charlie. We might be able to find you something."

Sean's eyes widened. "I didn't mean *here*. I mean, that

would be perfect, but I meant in general. You know everyone in town. I wasn't asking you specifically—"

Justin held up a hand. "You're a mechanic, Sean. You and I've been tinkering with engines since we could see over the hood. I can't hire people, but I'll talk to him."

A huge smile spread over Sean's face, taking ten years off. He resembled a giddy kid again. "Man, that would be great. Jayden is letting me work at her place on the weekends, you know, fixing up the house, but it's not enough hours. It would be so cool to work with you—*for* you. Thanks, bro."

Justin chuckled. "Don't thank me yet. You know Charlie. He's not going to hire you just because I ask him to." The two guys talked for a moment more before Justin had to get back to work rebuilding a motor. Sean stuck around and lent a hand, catching up and reminiscing about old times before their lives were so complicated.

It was enough to keep his mind off Holly…for that day.

Tonight marked the third date with Ben, and Holly was nervous as she slipped into her favorite little black dress. The soft black fabric hugged her curves and showed enough skin to make her feel elegant not trashy. Silver heels and a matching clutch, *check*. A bit of red lipstick, *check*. Hair flowing in curls down her back, straight from a shampoo commercial, *check*. Tonight, she simply wanted to enjoy Ben, same as their last couple of dates.

Their first dinner was nice, but of course, full of the first-date jitters. Their second date had been the silliest shenanigans; going bowling and playing putt-putt. Holly had laughed and had a great time, especially when Ben drove her home and they doted over the 'Cuda until he spent twenty minutes kissing her goodnight against the hood.

There was nothing holding her back from cultivating

a real relationship with Ben. Maybe now she could move on, be content, experience something new—some*one* new.

"How do I look, cat?" she asked the mass of fur that had run under her bed when she had turned the blow dryer on. All she received in return was a growl. Typical male.

Right on time, Ben knocked on the door. His face went slack as his eyes traveled over Holly, from her mass of golden curls to her silver heels and back again.

"Damn." He blew out a deep breath and Holly felt sexier than ever.

"I should say the same." She messed with the collar of his pressed white button-up that flowed nicely into grey slacks. "You clean up nice."

"You clean up like a diamond. Wow." He scrubbed a hand over his face. "I'm a lucky son of a gun." He slid a hand around her waist and pulled her close, bent down, and tenderly kissed her lips.

"I need to get back to the gym. This dress wasn't this tight the last time I wore it." She blushed and rubbed her hands over her thighs.

"I can't imagine it fitting any more perfect than it does right now."

"Thanks, Ben."

He guided her out to the car and opened the door for her, helping her slide into the leather-clad interior. They drove into the heart of Dalton, to the best Italian place in town. The chef was world-renowned and Ben loved authentic Italian food, as she found out on their first date.

"When my family comes to town," Holly said as they parked, "they always want to eat here at least once. It's so delicious. You're going to love it."

Ben took her hand and led her down the sidewalk. "I

can't believe I've never been here. But, then again, since I moved here last year, I've been working like a maniac, getting settled in, you know, learning the ins and outs of a new city."

"I completely know what you mean. I did the same thing when I moved here." Holly had made the reservations, hoping to surprise Ben with her selection. She kindly approached the hostess, "Reservations for Combs, please."

The young lady smiled. "Right this way." They walked towards the back of the restaurant and the hostess called over her shoulder, "Most of your party is already here."

"I'm sorry?" Her reservations were for two. How many bloody people had they written down, twenty? The hostess led them to the back of the restaurant then stepped aside, waving her arm at the table of people. Holly's breath expelled from her lungs as if she'd been kicked in the chest by a mule.

There sat her brother, Bear, Marshall, a couple other guys, and...*Justin.*

They made eye contact and he seemed to have been kicked by the same mule.

"Honeycomb!"

"Holly!"

Her childhood friends appeared delighted to see her, all but Justin and her brother.

"Wh-what are you guys doing here?" Holly said, attempting to act cool, but giving Hunter a pointed glare.

"It's my birthday." Bear stood up, towering over her, and stretched out his arms for a hug. "And you are a sight for sore eyes, Honeycomb. Get your fine ass over here and give me some love. Happy birthday to me. I didn't know you were coming."

Bear always coaxed a smile from her. He was aptly nicknamed. At well over six feet tall, built wide and strong, Jake Harris stood a head above the crowd. No one would ever miss him, especially with his sexy shoulder-length blond hair, bright blue eyes, wide smile, and overall rugged delicious looks.

Holly let him wrap his huge arms around her. "Neither did I, but happy birthday, Bear."

"Oh." His voice fell. "You have a friend."

"Huh? Oh! Yes, this is my…friend, Ben." Holly straightened as the other men at the table stood to greet them. It only seemed fitting that introductions began with her twin brother, who had just solidified the top spot on her shit-list. She had divulged earlier that week that she was coming to this restaurant tonight. "Ben, this is my brother, Hunter."

In his usual cocky attitude, Hunter held out his hand. "Hunter Combs. Nice to meet you, Ben."

They shook hands. "You too, man. Nice to meet some of Holly's family. You two look so much alike."

"We're twins," Holly and Hunter said in unison, something they had often done since childhood.

Ben grinned and nodded. "I see that."

She forced a smile and lifted her chin. "Ben, this is Bear Harris, Marshall Miller, and Bo, I presume?" Holly had never met Tina's fiancé in person, but there were pictures on social media and this guy was exactly what Tina described. Real short hair, kind eyes, muscles, tattoos.

The guy stood, his face pleasant and his smile gentle. "Bo Galloway. You must be Holly. It's real nice to meet you, ma'am."

"You too." Holly turned to Ben, who was shaking hands with the guys as she introduced them. "My friend Tina I told you is getting married; this is her fiancé."

"Oh, congrats, man. Holly mentioned how excited she is for the both of you." Ben was being super polite and it helped ease the awkwardness of the moment. The table separated him and Bo, so they both leaned in to shake hands. "Marriage is a huge step; I wish you the best."

"Thanks." Bo kept his smile.

Holly and Justin locked eyes and she saw the pain there. It squeezed her chest.

The other couple of guys worked with Bear or were buddies from Riverview. They worked their way around the table and back to Justin, who sat beside Hunter. What the hell was she going to say? How did she introduce him?

Her hands were sweating and her breaths weren't retrieving enough oxygen. Justin made no move to shake hands, as usual. He kept his hands in his pockets. If she had to guess, Justin still had a habit of hiding his fingernails because of the set-in stains from grease and oils he used at his shop.

"Sean." Bear waved a hand in the air. Holly turned and hardly recognized Bear's little brother. Sean was sober and bright-eyed for the first time in two years. He held a present as he made his way to the table.

Sean's brows rose as he saw Holly. "Honeycomb? Hey, beautiful! Long time no see."

"You too, little brother." Holly hugged him tight, thankful for whatever had straightened him out. "You look better, Sean." She pulled back and framed his face with her hands. The sight of him so healthy brought tears to her eyes. "Glad you're back."

Using the distraction to her advantage, Holly did a quick introduction and gingerly pushed Ben backwards.

"We're going to go get our table and leave you guys to it. Happy birthday, Bear. I love you dearly. Hunter, I'll call you later. Have fun, guys!" Holly pushed Ben a little harder, as he was trying to say individual goodbyes.

Justin's lips settled into a thin line and his eyes narrowed. But Holly didn't stop her retreat.

The hostess realized her mistake and set them up with a table for two across the restaurant. "Here you are. Sorry for the mistake. It's not every day we have two reservations under a name like Combs." She blushed and kept eyeing Ben.

"No problem," Ben said, flashing his dazzling smile. He seated Holly. "I got to meet your brother, *twin* brother. How coincidental that your friends from Riverview would be in Dalton tonight?"

"Not so much." Holly rubbed her temple. "My brother and I talk almost daily. He knew I wanted to bring you here." She tried to focus on Ben, but her mind was on Justin, sitting less than fifty feet away. "I figure Hunter wanted to meet you too, you know?" Holly glanced to their left, where the guys all laughed and had a fun time. "Typical brother antics."

Ben nodded. "I get it. I have a sister and a brother who are always planning trouble for me."

"Such as?" Holly unfolded her napkin in her lap and used all her willpower to focus on Ben as he prattled on about his sister, the lawyer, and his brother, the neurosurgeon. He came from a stable family, a family of smart, well-educated, and highly motivated people.

Mom would love that.

They ordered wine and entrées. Ben's sexy smile distracted her for a few minutes, and when he reached across the table to intertwine their fingers, Holly felt a wave of guilt and desire fighting for her attention.

While they waited, Bo approached the table. "Holly? Sorry to intrude," he said to Ben, who graciously waved it off. "I told T that I ran into you and she wanted to come visit sometime this next weekend. Is that okay?" Bo glanced at his phone, as if he was ready to dictate her answer.

And they had to interrupt my date to ask this question?

Holly nodded. "Sure. Yeah. Have her call me…later. Tomorrow?" She shifted her eyes to Ben and Bo nodded.

"Yeah, of course. Enjoy your meal." He left and Holly cast Ben an apologetic grimace.

"Sorry. Knowing Tina, she told him to come over here *right* now." Holly rolled her eyes and took Ben's hand again. "So how about you tell me what we are going to do tomorrow night?"

"Tomorrow night?" Ben's face lit up. "Two dates in one weekend. Can we handle that?"

"I imagine we can." Holly felt heat rise up her neck.

As soon as they were deep in conversation about Holly's days modeling in college, Bear came to their table. He didn't bother apologizing for intruding. He even grabbed a chair from another table and sat with them.

Holly gaped at him. "Can I help you?"

Bear smiled innocently and turned to Ben. "So, Ben, Hunter said you're a firefighter? My younger brother was a firefighter too. You work here in town?"

Amused, Ben chuckled and engaged Bear in a five-minute discussion about which department he worked for and how he and Holly met.

"Forgive me being nosy. Holly's a little sister to me, and I don't get to see her often, so I have to pull the big brother routine when I can." Bear winked at Holly.

"That's great." Ben nodded. "I'm the same way with my little sister. I'm glad that Holly has people watching out for her."

"And Holly would appreciate those people watching from a distance," Holly said with a little sass and a fake smile.

Both the guys laughed. Their food arrived and Bear had the decency to leave them alone and let them eat.

"You don't have to be embarrassed." Ben took a drink of his wine. "It's pretty funny. They're all hazing me."

Holly's shoulders dropped. "Thank you for being so understanding." She bit into her alfredo chicken and sighed with happiness. "This is divine."

"Mine's really tasty too. Here, try it." He forked some of his pasta and fed it to her. Ben's eyes stayed on her lips as they closed around the fork. He licked his lips and Holly felt a tingle in her lower stomach. "Damn, that was a lot sexier than I anticipated. Speaking of sexy, have I told you how beautiful you are tonight?"

Holly finished her bite, blushing. "You did. But you can tell me again."

Ben winked at her and started talking about a training that he was leading the next week. He was excited about it.

Holly glanced over her left shoulder and saw Justin laughing with their friends. His eyes shifted to hers and the smile fell from his face. It raked at her insides when he turned away and ignored her.

"Holly?"

"Hmm?" She turned to Ben.

"Want to join them? It's fine, really. They seem great—"

"No!" She emphatically shook her head and coughed,

then wiped her mouth with her napkin. "I don't want to have to share you, not tonight."

Wow, that came out more romantic than I planned.

Ben's face darkened with desire. He leaned over the table and took her hand. "I don't want to share you either. In fact, I'd prefer to get our check and take you back to my place for dessert." He brought her knuckles to his lips.

Across the restaurant, there was some commotion. Holly and Ben turned to see Justin standing in the corner with his drink spilled down his shirt and pants. He cussed and wiped at the spill, his eyes flickering to her for a second before darting away.

Luckily, he said something she couldn't hear, everyone laughed, and he sat back down.

Holly quickly tried to bring Ben's attention back to her. "Ignore them. All that matters tonight is right here." She flagged down the waiter and ordered another round of wine.

The rest of their meal went without distraction and Holly almost forgot about the stalkers in the corner. As the sun went down and the lights dimmed, a pianist played the baby grand in the opposite corner of the restaurant. That helped pull her attention away from the guys.

"Dance with me?" Ben extended his hand and gave her that panty-dropping smile that was so infectious.

Holly took his hand and let him lead her onto the dance floor for a slow number. They swayed from side to side, not quite finding the right beat of the song. Holly tried to gently lead their movements, but Ben was so tall and busy talking that he didn't pay attention to the beats. Oddly, it annoyed her.

"You never have explained why you don't live in

Riverview with your family. You and your brother are close, right?"

"We are," Holly agreed quickly. "But…have you ever had something happen and it opened your eyes to things you never realized before?"

Ben nodded, his face turning serious. "Yeah, I get that."

"That's what happened for me. Suddenly, everything that I had in Riverview—who I was in Riverview—none of it felt safe anymore. Not that Riverview ever changed, but—"

"You did," Ben finished her sentence. "I totally understand. That's why I'm in Dalton too. My last girlfriend ended up sleeping with one of my co-workers. We had alternate shifts and while I was fighting fires, she was starting them…with him. Months after it all came out, the whole department still talked about it in hushed voices." His shoulders moved up and down. "It was difficult to stay there. So I transferred up here."

Holly could relate. For weeks after Lance's death, people still whispered behind her back as she walked through the grocery store. It drove her nuts. Unlike Hunter, who blew off what most people said about him, Holly was a people-pleaser and, though they shouldn't, their opinions affected her. "I, um, I lost someone. It was tragic and I guess I never got over it."

Whether she was talking about losing Lance or losing Justin, she honestly didn't know. In many ways, she lost three people the night Lance drove them off the road and into the Sanguine River. Lance, Justin, and herself. The truth of that night haunted her still and it was the main reason she had trouble facing her friends. Nearly four years later, she still woke up in the middle of the night gasping for breath, the fear of drowning fogging her mind and causing panic attacks.

"May I cut in?" Holly jerked back and there stood Hunter. Even if her brother was conniving tonight, he was still her brother and her twin, a bond that could never be broken, not even by his asinine antics.

"Absolutely." Ben bowed out and shook Hunter's hand. "Your sister is amazing. I'm lucky to be here with her."

"I agree on both points." Hunter cordially returned the handshake and then swept Holly up into a waltz. "Enjoying your date?"

"I'm trying to." Holly easily kept in step with his movements. They had years of dance classes together, insuring they were the entertainment of their mother's ritzy Hollywood parties. Hunter had become a fabulous dancer, a man fluid on his feet with masculine grace. It made the ladies swoon…once they found out he was straight.

"Are you also trying to break Justin into a million pieces?" His eyes met hers and she could see the concern over his friend.

Holly sighed. "It's over between us, Hunt. It has been for a long time; we just haven't put it in writing. Besides, he doesn't love me anymore. He can barely stand the sight of me."

"He can barely look at you because he's so jealous, he's about to explode."

Holly scoffed. "Jealousy isn't love. If he wanted me so damn badly, why didn't he come get me? And while we're asking questions, why did you bring all of them here tonight? I told you about my date and you used it against me."

Hunter's jaw tensed and he hesitated before he spoke. "Holly, you're the most important person in my life.

Justin is my best friend and it might be the biggest secret in Riverview, but you two are *married*." He said the word through gritted teeth. "That makes him my brother. I care about both of you and this has gone on long enough. He's never moved on, Honey. He still loves you. I know you love him too."

Holly frowned. "It's not enough. You don't understand, Hunt. It's not him I've been running from. It never was."

Her brother's brows dipped and he pinched his lips together. "Then what? Who?"

The song ended and Holly kissed his cheek. "Later. Not tonight." She smiled and tried not to let the emotion overtake her. She loved Hunter more than any one person on the planet, but now was not the time or the place to exorcise her ghosts. "Celebrate Bear's birthday. We can hash this out later."

Hunter sighed and held her hands. "It's always later with you, Holly. You're always avoiding the issues. But time is running out. You're about to lose the best thing that ever happened to you." He kissed her cheek and walked away, his jaws clenched tight.

His words stung and made her chest constrict until it was painful to breathe. Was that who she had become? The perpetual avoider? Tina accused her of the same thing; burying her head in the sand. Maybe they were right.

Ben shook his head as she came back to the table. "I had no idea you could dance. You two have done this many times, haven't you?"

She cast a glance to her brother's table. "Hunter and I do the same old dance far too often."

Holly truly studied Ben for the first time. Such a genuinely nice guy. So handsome and full of joy. All she had to do was allow herself to be his and there was a high probability he could make her happy.

Justin's voice rang out in her mind and she was transported back in time to a night her senior year when they lay on the roof of his house wrapped in a blanket. Justin had already graduated and was simply waiting for her so they could get married. *No one can make you happy, Honey. You must take life as it comes and craft your own happiness. That's why we need each other, because I remind you to seize your happiness, and being with you is seizing my happiness. If you need to go to college in Carreyville, if that is what fulfills you, I'll wait. I love you, Holly. Always have, always will.*

"You okay?" Ben pulled her chair out.

There she stood, lost in a memory. What the hell was she doing here? Why was she on a date with this guy when the love of her life sat across the restaurant? Holly reached for her purse. "I'm going to go to the ladies' room. Be right back."

"Are you okay?" Ben touched her cheek. He glanced over towards the table with the guys. "You want to get out of here?"

Holly sighed, thankful for his sense of observation. "I—I don't know. Can I have a moment? I'm sorry." Maybe she could kindly break it off with Ben before they reached the car and still come back for Justin.

"Don't apologize, cutie-pie. I got it." He waved the waiter down as she went to the restroom.

Not that she needed to go; she simply needed a moment to collect her thoughts.

No such luck. Justin came out of the men's room and they froze in the narrow hall. *Shit.*

As many times as Holly had laid her eyes on Justin over

their lives, each time copied the first. He stole her breath. It was his eyes. Those deep, rich, hazel eyes that belonged to an old soul. They pierced into her, seeing too much, seeing everything. She had fallen in love with those eyes as a teenager and stayed in love with those eyes until the night she feared what they would see.

Justin didn't have a traditionally handsome face like Hunter or even Ben. He was rougher, rawer. He kept scruff on his jaw, which only accentuated his full lips. Those lips had brought her great pleasure at one time.

Now his eyes and his lips both created a pinched expression of anger. "You didn't introduce me."

Holly took a deep breath. "And how would that go, exactly? Introducing my date to my…husband?" She hardly whispered the word, yet it felt like a scream, a billboard announcing it to the world. Guilt cultivated like sickness in her chest.

"We can easily alter that." His eyes dropped to the floor. "It's just paper."

"It's not."

Anger flashed like lightning in his eyes as they met hers. "You're on a damn date, Holly. Don't tell me it's not just a piece of paper. You gave up on us years ago and now," he scrubbed a hand down his face, squeezing his eyes closed in pain, "so have I." He pushed past her.

"Justin." Her heart sank and shattered. All this time, she held on to that link to Justin. Like there was still a chance he would come around and she would run to him and confess everything and they would work it out.

"I'll mail the papers, Holly. My lawyer already has them drawn up." He went back to the table and Holly followed him.

She grabbed for his arm. "Justin, please. This isn't right. What can I do?"

He rounded on her. "What can you…what can you do?" His eyes narrowed and he scoffed. "I'm tired of being alone. I'm tired of grasping for the little bread crumbs of hope. I'm tired of filing my damn taxes as married but separate." His voice rose with every sentence. "I'm tired of feeling guilty when I meet someone and consider dating. I'm tired of feeling pathetic because my own *wife* doesn't want me. And I'm tired of living with a dream that will never come true. What can you do? You can sign the divorce papers and stay the hell out of my life!"

Time stopped. The world quit spinning as Justin screamed those words at her.

Everything froze. Chatter of other patrons. The sound of the piano.

Holly glanced over her shoulder to see they had the attention of the entire restaurant…*no*…including the guys at her brother's table…*oh God*…and Ben…*please, God, this isn't happening*…whose brows reached high on his forehead.

Bear, Marshall, Sean—all the guys who had no idea that Holly and Justin were married—now picked their jaws up off the floor.

Oh God. I can't breathe.

Panic filled her and the room spun out of control. *Please, not a panic attack! Not now.* Her lungs felt like caves, an expanse so large, she couldn't fill them with air no matter how hard she breathed. She grabbed for the wall and closed her eyes, hoping like hell the dizziness would subside and that she didn't fall out on the floor in the middle of the restaurant.

Hunter, who had witnessed many of her attacks, must've recognized her symptoms. He came to her side and grabbed her elbow.

Justin cursed and rubbed his temple. "I need some air."

Hunter nodded to him and stood in front of Holly to block her from the prying eyes of the onlookers. "Back up, into the hallway."

Holly gasped for breath, stumbled, but did as instructed. Her fingertips began to tingle and her toes went cold. The small hallway constricted, shrinking down and getting darker.

"Deep breaths, Holly. Breathe."

Holly closed her eyes and tried to focus on her breaths. Through a long, hollow tunnel, she heard Ben's voice.

What's wrong with her?

She's having a panic attack.

How can I help?

Grab that chair. She needs to sit, but she won't want people gawking at her.

Hunter gently sat her in the chair and urged her to put her head down to get her blood flowing again. He knelt in front of her. "Focus on your breathing. Stretch your fingers."

Holly gripped his hands. Her blurry eyes met his. "I'm sorry, Hunt. I've ruined your party. I'm sorry. I'm sorry." Apologies spilled out of her lips. This mentally deranged person she became during a panic attack was her worst fear. No one wanted to see this side of her, the broken, fearful, out-of-control side. Her body shook and tears rolled down her cheeks. "I didn't mean to. I'm sorry, Hunt. Forgive me. I'm sorry."

"Honey." He sighed and dropped a kiss on her forehead. "It's my fault."

Ben came closer. "Should I take her home?"

"I can, if you would rather not." Hunter glanced up.

"It's not my style to leave my dates. The waitress is getting our check. Besides, we obviously have some things to talk about." Ben gave Hunter a half smile.

"Look, man, my sister might not be in the right frame of mind to—"

"It's fine." Holly stood, grabbed the wall, and steadied herself. "Get me out of here."

Hunter put his arm around her waist. "Holly, you don't have to—"

"I can't do this. Not in front of so many people. Get me out of here."

Hunter nodded. "Okay, Honey. Y'all go on. I'll take care of the check." He helped her out of the hallway.

Holly's heart broke into even smaller pieces as she met Bear's eyes. His lips pinched into a thin, sympathetic smile. He lifted a hand but then dropped it when Holly shook her head and kept walking.

Stay away, Bear. I hurt everyone around me.

Neither Ben nor Holly said a word as they drove back to her cabin. Ben parked his car in the driveway and turned off the engine. They sat in silence. Neither moved and Holly didn't want to breathe.

"You're married," Ben whispered.

"Separated. Divorcing."

"I heard."

She flinched. "Ben, I'm so sorry."

"Do you still love him?"

"We've been separated for years; I don't know why we

didn't file sooner."

Ben turned in his seat to face her. "Do you still love him?"

Holly's eyes clamped shut and opened her mouth twice before she answered, "I don't *not* love him."

"There's nothing wrong with still being in love with your husband, Holly. If you want to save your marriage, by all means, go. Be honest about it. I'm a big boy and I happen to believe in the sanctity of marriage. Do you still love him?" He accentuated his question with staccato beats.

Holly wiped her tears and nodded. "Yes. I thought I could quit, move on, fall for someone else—someone wonderful like you." She huffed and stared out the window.

"You love who you love. Don't be ashamed of it."

"Ben." Holly reached of his hand. "I'm sorry. I should've never gotten you mixed up in my drama. This is why I don't usually date. My life is so complicated."

"You tried to move on, Holly. We talked about this, remember."

"Stop. Stop being so nice and honorable." Her head fell backwards.

Ben laughed darkly. "Listen, cutie-pie. I'm trying hard here. Part of me says you need someone to take your mind off your ex and I can take you in that house right now and do it."

"Not the worst idea I've heard all night." Holly grinned, trying to lighten the mood. "The other part?"

Ben kissed her hand as it held his and gazed deep into her eyes. "The other part of me wishes that my ex would've loved me enough to fight for me, for what we had. I've been in Justin's shoes." He dropped his face. "I might be a god-damned fool for letting you go, but I'd be an even bigger fool for getting in the middle of a marriage."

"I'm—"

"Don't." His tone hardened and he held out a hand to stop her words. "Go inside, Holly."

Tears welled up in her eyes, but she slid out of his car and watched as he drove away. Once inside, Holly kicked off her heels, removed her jewelry, and exchanged her pretty dress for spandex pants. As she sat on her couch, Unnamed-Ugly cat crawled up and sat beside her. He didn't touch her, didn't face her. He just sat there.

Not for the first time, her cabin was too lonely, too quiet. The constant sound of running water called out to her. Holly grabbed the cat and a bottle of rum, meandered down the pier, kicked off her shoes, and dangled her feet into the water. Against his wishes, she held the fur ball in her lap as she drank straight from the bottle.

Holly both loved and hated this river. It held so many memories, so many more secrets. There had been parties at the swimming hole, full of laughter and joy. There was the one night she and Justin had snuck into the park and went to the not-so-secret make-out spot. She lost more than her bathing suit bottoms that night.

That memory burned in her chest, hotter than the alcohol, opening a chasm of longing.

Her best memories in the Sanguine involved Justin and their friends.

In her worst memories, much like tonight, she was alone. The night Lance had died, she sat on the bank of the river for over an hour, alone, waiting on the old man to turn his truck around and go home to call an ambulance. She had never felt lonelier than she did as she watched the headlights of Lance's car disappear beneath the water and eventually fade to blackness.

Even now, she had no one. There was no one to call and talk to about her secrets, no shoulder to cry on.

And whose fault is that? She wiped angrily at her tears.

Holly glanced down to the feline eyes that observed her. "I push everyone away. No wonder only an ugly-ass cat loves me."

On cue, the fur ball grumbled in argument. He had had enough affection and scrambled to get out of her hold.

Not even the damn cat liked her. He only stayed because she fed him.

Bastard.

Once her friends knew the truth, knew what she had been keeping from them, they would never forgive her. Tina, Jayden, Keri, Meg…they would be so upset once they realized who she was on the inside.

Justin hated her.

Hunter was probably angry with her for making a scene.

She put Hunter and Justin in a place where they had to come clean to their friends.

And I ruined Bear's birthday. No wonder I'm alone.

Holly sank deep in her pity party and cried, picking at the label of her rum bottle. Pathetic. Her life was simply pathetic. Justin would be better off without her. They all would be.

Tears flowed heavily and fell into the river. Maybe it would carry them downstream all the way to Riverview, all the way to Justin and the friends she missed.

A gust of chilly air sent shivers down her spine and she figured since her vision had grown a little fuzzy, she should probably go inside. Holly tightened the lid on her bottle, set it on the pier beside her, and struggled to get to her feet. Captain Morgan whipped her ass harder than her initial assessment. She closed her eyes and tried to steady herself.

It didn't work.

Cold water slapped her in the face a second later.

Holly grasped for the surface, wide awake as her brain managed to kick into survival mode. Her head broke the surface and she coughed, gasping for air. Bobbing in the water, floating swiftly away, was her bottle of rum.

"Take it," she screamed at the river. "Take it like you take everything, you heartless bastard!" She swam for the pier and pulled herself out of the water, cussing and grumbling as she dragged her soggy butt into the house.

There was a hint of something stinky in the air, something she hadn't noticed earlier. She stripped her clothes and grabbed a towel, surveying her house to find the source of the smell.

The cat sat proudly in a corner next to a grey lump. Upon closer inspection, Holly grimaced and moaned. *Perfect.*

A mangled corpse of what might've been a mole lay on her floor for her viewing pleasure. That damn cat strutted around, circling his prize with the attitude of a runway model.

"I can't believe you're proud of this. It's gross." She cleaned up his kill and disposed of the body. *Yuck.*

Tired and cold to the bone, she collapsed on the couch.

A screech that rivaled nails on a chalkboard came from below. The crap-colored fur ball hopped up right in her lap, a welcoming committee of ugly. This was the first time he'd willingly shown her any affection. He still stank, despite the soapy water she tried to dunk him in.

"You're like a public bathroom, ya know?" She tentatively ran her hand over his back and he arched under her touch. "No matter how much air freshener you spray, it ends up smelling of flowers and pooh."

The cat, seemingly pleased that she was interacting, purred and settled on her lap. It was an odd comfort after the last couple days away from home. Holly laid her head back on the couch and closed her eyes, soothed by the rhythmic purrs of her companion.

He needs a name.

Ugly Bastard might describe him best, but she couldn't very well name him that. Mole Killing Bastard didn't roll off the tongue. Rat Killing Bastard wasn't much better. Rat Bastard…R…B…Arby. She chuckled and made eye contact with the cat. "Welcome home, Arby."

Right as her body loosened and relaxed, someone knocked on her door, scaring the bejesus out of her and Arby both.

Knock. Knock. Knock.

Who could possibly be at her door, besides perhaps Hunter? Had her brother come to bitch her out?

Knock. Knock. Knock.

"I'm coming." Holly opened the door and gasped.

The visitor turned her head of flaming red hair and removed a pair of wide sunglasses, exposing a hellova shiner. Her busted lip pulled back into a sad smile. "Hi, Holly."

"Megs."

Meg tilted her head. "Why are you naked?"

"**Y**OU TWO ARE FREAKIN' *MARRIED*? AND YOU NEVER told us?" Bear griped loudly as the guys paid their tab and left the restaurant. "I can't believe you kept something like this from *us*."

Justin groaned. Not his best moment. They had an hour and half drive back to Riverview and he cringed, knowing what would be the primary topic of discussion. "We never told anyone."

"Was she pregnant?" Marshall asked in hushed tone.

"No!" Justin waved him off. "We got married and while she was still in the process of breaking it off with Lance. Then he had his wreck and died. She didn't handle it well. She left. I've never been able to get her back."

"You guys have been brothers-in-law all this time." Bo wiggled his finger between Hunter and Justin. Both nodded. Bo let out a huff and shook his head.

"And you can't talk sense into your sister?" Marshall nudged Hunter's shoulder.

"She wouldn't listen." Those words didn't come from Hunter. They came from Sean, who absently gazed outside the window as they drove back to Riverview. "No matter how many people in my family tried to talk to me after Chris died, I never wanted to hear it. Guilt is a safe place to be. It's constant. Becomes your friend, your companion, your identity. It keeps you from doing things that would make you vulnerable to more pain. If you get close enough to your guilt, it shields you from feeling anything else."

"True that." Bo nodded his head.

The car was silent for a solid minute while they all digested that.

Justin cleared his throat. "I don't know why she feels so guilty. Not *that* guilty. I mean, I felt guilt, sure. Lance was mad at us for getting back together and that's why he was driving so crazy. But in the end, he made the choice to drive drunk and he paid the consequences."

"Maybe she doesn't see it that way," Bear said.

"Obviously, she doesn't." That still didn't explain her self-imposed banishment to Justin. Driving after drinking a bottle of whiskey and having a wreck seemed stupid on Lance's part. Cut and dry, right?

"Haven't you ever asked her?" Hunter's tone held enough accusation to cause Justin to get defensive.

"You're her twin brother. Haven't *you*?"

"She's never wanted to talk about it. Her answer is always to talk about it later. Later never comes. After a while, I quit asking."

"Listen," Bo said, rubbing the peach fuzz on the top of his head. "I know better than anyone that four years is a long time to convince yourself of just about anything. The first couple years I was in jail, I had convinced myself everything was my fault. No one else was a screw-up except for me. It wasn't until Nan forced me into anger management that I got some perspective. It sounds like the same story with this chick."

"Yep. Someone should ask her. Holly is clearly viewing Lance's death from a standpoint none of us have considered. She knows something we don't and it's severe enough for her to isolate herself from friends and family." Sean shrugged his shoulders when they all looked at him. "Just sayin'."

"Damn, Sean." Justin glanced over at their recently sobered friend. "Where'd all this deep thinking come from?"

Sean scoffed. "Amazing what your brain can do when it's not clouded with drugs and shit." The other guys chuckled. "And I've been seeing a head-shrinker. Mom's stipulation for moving back in. Holly should too."

Bear put his arm on the back of the seat around his brother. "I'm proud of you, bro."

"We all are," Justin agreed. At least one positive thing had come from tonight.

After all his friends left, Justin went for a jog through downtown and towards the river. The park had a great trail, open and lit up enough to be safe late at night. He didn't care about the time; he needed to work the anxiety out of his muscles.

As he ran, he thought about what Sean and Bo had said, how guilt took a person over and even made them believe things that weren't true. What had four years of guilt done to Holly? What recollections of that night did she have that he didn't understand?

Had he even been asking the right questions?

Why the hell had it taken him this long to wrap his head around the fact that Holly had obviously withheld information? It was awful enough that she would rather run than face it.

Justin pushed his body a little harder and made another lap around the park and ended up jogging beside the river. The more he thought about all the time he wasted trying to do what was best for Holly, the harder his feet hit the pavement.

Idiot. He might've lost her forever because he was too stupid to put the pieces together. All this time, *damn it!* He had yelled at her in public, made her have a panic attack, humiliated her. He'd told her to stay the hell out of his life. *Damn idiot!*

Justin went off trail and down by the water. He was out of breath and plopped down on his butt, right in the dirt. His chest heaved with exertion and aggravation. The flowing waters of the Sanguine caught his eyes and he stared into their black depths.

Damn river. Maybe he could blame it for his current predicament. The river took Lance, it nearly took Holly, and now, it was what stood between them. Miles of river ran between him and Holly and he didn't know if he would ever be able to cross it.

He had to make this right, to force Holly to describe precisely what was going on. Then he had to beg for her forgiveness.

Justin stared at the river so long, his rear-end started to go numb and he let out a long yawn. It would take a while to get back to his apartment. By then, he would be so exhausted, he could fall into bed and, hopefully, not dream of

Holly. Maybe he could grab a couple hours of sleep before the sun came up.

As he stood and dusted the dirt off his shorts, a flicker in the water caught his eye. The moonlight reflected off a glass bottle that was tangled in a tree root. He bent down and picked up a half empty bottle of Captain Morgan. The edges of the label were peeled off.

What the hell?

The bottle triggered a memory of Holly. They were sixteen and had snuck out of her house to go drinking by the river. They would kiss and sip rum, falling deeper and deeper in love as the river flowed by. She always peeled the edges of the labels off her bottles.

He opened the lid and took a sniff. Smelled okay. Not old or stale, almost like it was freshly opened. There wasn't anything growing around the lid, like most of the trash that had spent a lot of time in the water. The Sanguine could carry litter for miles in its current and there was no telling where the bottle had come from. It could've fallen out of a boat or washed away from a riverside camping trip.

Grinning to himself as he threw the bottle in the trash receptacle, he took it as a sign. It was time to get his woman back.

Holly threw her arms around Meg and both women cried. They had always been so close, even during their college years when they were apart. When Meg moved even further away, to Boston, it nearly killed Holly, as if part of her heart went too.

"What are you doing here?" Holly helped get her luggage inside, uncaring that she wore nothing but her undergarments and a towel. "What happened to your face? Why do you have so many suitcases?" Far too many for a quick weekend trip.

"I left him," Meg sobbed. "Cole hit me for the last time."

"He what!" Holly yelled. That was where the bruises came from. "The *last* time? You mean this wasn't the *first* time?"

Meg turned her face towards the light and revealed another ugly bruise on her jaw. "We were fighting for the umpteenth time about everything from who is supposed to pick up his dry cleaning to how horrid his mother is and I," she hiccupped, "I told him that I didn't love him, that I never loved him, and I wanted a divorce."

Holly guided Meg to the couch then ran to put on dry clothes. The cabin was small enough Meg could still be heard in the next room.

"Cole said that I was nothing but a slut and a worthless piece of shit. So I told him he was an impotent asshole with mommy-issues. Next thing I know, I'm on the ground and he's slapping my head, hitting my face with his fist. He even kicked me."

Holly slid on her shirt and came back into the living room. "Oh my God! Meg! Don't you need to go to a hospital?"

She shook her mass of red hair. "I already did. I filed charges and everything. The police came to arrest him and his mother threatened me. The cop told me to go someplace safe." Meg's bloodshot green eyes met Holly's. "I came to you. Cole doesn't know about your cabin. I've never talked about where you live. If he comes for me, he would go straight to Riverview, straight to my parents' house, or one of my siblings, or Tina even. But never here."

"Okay, that's smart. I'm glad you came, Megan. You're safe here." Holly hugged her close, tears streaming down her cheeks. God, she relived the past all over again. Only this time, she wasn't the scared victim. Holly related far too well to Meg in this situation and it might be a help.

"I'm sorry, Holly," Meg sobbed. "I'm sorry to bring you my troubles, but I didn't know where else to go. I was so scared. What if he gets out of jail? You know his mother is going to bail him out."

Holly shook her head, wondering how Meg had managed to keep it together long enough to get on a plane in Boston and come to Texas. She was already in a fragile state these days. Meg lost her older brother years ago, but recently, her toddler son, sweet baby Noah, had died from fibril seizures. He might have survived if Meg's piece of shit husband would have let her have a car…or use public transportation…or had a heart and common sense. But no. The hours that Meg had to wait for her husband to come home allowed an infection to incubate. They took Noah to the ER, but by then, the baby was much worse. Meg had used all her medical training to keep his fever down. It simply wasn't enough.

Can't fate be kinder to her for five freaking minutes?

And of all the places to run to, Meg had to run to the one person who only had more heartache and secrets that would hurt her.

That didn't matter tonight. Right now, Meg needed a friend to carry her burdens. "Listen, don't borrow that trouble. He would be a fool to come searching for you. Imagine what all our guy friends will do when they find out he hit you. I'm going to tell Hunter if he sees Cole in town to beat the snot out of him on sight."

"No!" Meg's eyes widened and she gripped Holly's shoulders. "Don't tell anyone I'm here. If you tell anyone, then word will get back to Bear and—"

"Bear?"

"—he'll do something crazy, because he hates Cole."

"Why does Bear hate Cole?" Holly missed a piece of the puzzle somewhere.

Out of nowhere, Meg screamed and jumped up on the couch as a little grey streak raced under her feet, and a scraggly brown fur ball right after it.

Not knowing what had played tag on her toes, Holly screamed bloody murder and leapt on the couch too.

"What the hell is that?" Meg threw out her hand and pointed to the kitchen. "It's in there!"

Holly heard a screech and hissing and her trash can fell over. *Rat bastard cat.* She groaned and stepped off the couch. "It's a cat." She reached for the broom in case his prey was still alive and she had to kill it.

"You don't like cats."

"I don't." Holly peeked around the cabinets to see the cat batting his paw at a dead mouse and making a low growling noise. "I absolutely freaking do *not* like cats. This one won't leave."

The dead mouse pulled a Lazarus, rolled over, popped up, and ran right for Holly, the cat hot on his furry heels. Holly screamed the most pathetic, girly, wussy scream and vaulted over the edge of the couch.

It took her a second to realize that Meg was laughing at her, hard. She had a hand over her mouth, but it didn't hold back her amusement.

"It's not funny, bitch."

Holly's indignation only made Meg bray with laughter until she joined in.

"You got your ass handed to you by a mouse." Megan's sad tears had turned into tears of silliness and she gripped her waist as she flopped down on the couch.

"Shut up." Holly grabbed a couch cushion and threw it at Meg but giggled at her lack of courage in the face of a tiny little field mouse.

Arby came sauntering by with the limp mouse in his mouth. He glanced over at Holly and let out a weird huffing noise, as if to mock her.

"Did you see that?" Holly's mouth hung open and Meg covered her fresh bout of laughter with the pillow.

"Holy crap, your cat is mocking you."

"He's not my cat. He's a little rat bastard stalker." Holly curled up on the couch opposite Meg.

"Says the woman with cat food in the corner."

"Whatever." Holly rolled her eyes but grinned.

Their laughter slowly died down. "I'm glad you came here, Megs."

Meg's lips pulled back and she crawled over to lay her head on Holly's shoulder. "Me too, Honey."

The girls stayed up talking until the wee hours of the morning. Holly simply allowed Meg to vent for hours about Cole, his awful mother, and their years of strained marriage, the pain she endured at losing her son. There was so much that Meg dealt with over the years. All their friends shared a disdain for Cole. He had subjected Meg to mental and emotional abuse, neglecting her basic needs, and trampling on her desire to put her nursing certificate to work. In Cole's eyes, it was her duty to stay home, raise the kids, and keep the house, and have dinner ready by six; exactly as his mother had done for his father.

"That's not what I signed up for, you know? Then Noah came along and all I wanted was to be his mom."

"I thought Cole was kind to Noah?"

"He was," Megan said quickly. "Not at first. Infancy was hard for Cole. Bottles and multiple feedings in the middle of the night, diapers and doctor visits. After Noah started cooing and showing signs of a personality, not even Cole resisted him." Her eyes focused on nothing, her mind on a pain that dwelt deep inside her. "Cole's mother fell in love with him and that eased the relationship a little."

"Of course." Holly rubbed her arm. "That was her grandbaby. How could she not love him?"

Meg's eyes met hers for a second and then darted away. "Yeah, right, of course." She uncurled herself from the couch. "I hate to be a bum, but I've had a hell of a day. What do you say I keep your couch from walking off tonight and, uh, we continue this in the morning?"

"Sure, anything you need." Holly rose and moved some of the decorative pillows off the couch. "I'll grab you some blankets."

Before Holly left Meg to sleep, she hugged her again, still in shock that she was there. "I love you, Megs. I'm glad you came here."

"You've always been there for me, Holly. You, Tina, Jayden, Keri. I can't imagine getting through this last year without all of you. I love you too."

"Get some sleep. We'll take on the world's problems tomorrow." Holly retreated to her room, followed by Arby, who laid claim to a corner of her bed.

Of all the possible outcomes of tonight, Holly hadn't seen any of this coming. All she had planned was a nice, quiet dinner with Ben and that had gone right down the shitter. Justin's outburst, Ben's break-up, falling in the river, now Meg's arrival. *Whew.* She let out a deep breath.

Needing to do one last thing before bed, Holly picked up her phone and saw many missed text messages.

Ben: *Sorry things went down like this. I wish you the best.*

Hunter: *Are you okay? Do I need to kill a firefighter... and my brother-in-law?*

Sean: *If you want to talk, I'm here for you.*

And finally, one that made her chest constrict, Justin, a few moments ago, at nearly four in the morning: *We need to talk. Sorry I yelled, but it's time to get things straight.*

What did that mean? What would they possibly talk about at this point? Holly replied to each of them.

Ben: *Thanks, and again, sorry.*

Hunter: *I can't afford bail money and you're too pretty to go to prison. But thanks for the offer. Don't tell a soul, Meg is here. I'll explain later.*

Sean: *Thanks. So nice to see you.*

Justin: *You hurt me tonight. But I've hurt you for years. Yes, we need to talk.*

Justin's reply was swift. *I'll be there Sunday. Good night…morning.*

He didn't leave room for negotiation. If she were honest with herself, that was for the best. Holly excelled at putting people off, procrastinating, and avoiding confrontation. Now her time had run out.

As frightened and anxious as it made her, Holly needed to start with Meg. She had to explain exactly what happened the night Lance died and pray that Meg forgave her for the role she played in his death.

⁕

Cold water, rushing over my face. I'm going to drown. I'm going to die.

Justin, help!

There's no air. I can't breathe. So much water. I'm sinking.

Get out. Through the window. Get out or die.

Where is Lance? I can't reach him. He's dead.

Air. I need air. There's no air. Don't take a breath.

Kick off the car. Swim to the surface. Hurry. Fight the

current.

Swim harder. I need air. Lance is still in the water.

Air! I can breathe! Thank God, I can breathe.

Holly gasped for breath as she flew upright in bed. Her hand reaching out to the ceiling, searching the surface of the water. *Air!*

Blinking, she came fully awake. This made the fourth panic attack in a month. She put her feet on the floor and bent to lower her head between her knees.

Calm down. Breathe. Nothing has happened yet. Meg will understand; she just went through this with Cole. She'll get it.

Once the tingling in her fingertips subsided and the shadows in her vision ceased, Holly slowly stood and stretched, trying to get her blood flowing the right way. There had to be a way to deal with this. Maybe it was time to see a doctor. Too many mornings started this way and it left her in a funk.

Meg's here. A realization that both excited and frightened her.

The scent of bacon hit her nose and drew her out of her bedroom like a siren.

Meg stood in the kitchen cooking, her beautiful red hair bundled in an unruly, curly mass on the top of her head. She took a tiny piece of bacon and offered it to the cat. "Here you go, kitty-kitty." She offered a compassionate smile. "You're about the mangiest little thing, aren't you? Poor baby." Arby purred under her petting hand. "Aww. Sweet boy, or girl, I don't know."

"Boy," Holly said, entering the kitchen as Meg held Arby up to confirm. "His name is Arby."

"You've never liked animals much. I'm surprised at

this." Meg set the cat down and turned back to her cooking.

"You and me both." Holly rubbed her pulsing temple.

"I hope you don't mind me taking over your kitchen. I wasn't hungry at all yesterday and I know I need to eat something. Coffee is ready."

"You made coffee?" *Thank you, Jesus.* "Say no more, the kitchen is officially yours."

"Coffee, bacon, and biscuits and eggs."

Holly sighed with happiness and hugged Meg from behind. "Damn, I'm glad you're here."

Meg giggled, her voice soft and high. "Me too. And um, speaking of that." She turned to face Holly.

Seeing her busted lip and black eye cooked up hatred within Holly. She wanted to tell all their big-brother friends about what Cole had done and watch them unleash their fury all over him. It made her want to scream "Unleash the Kraken!" and revel in victory as Cole got the tar beat out of him. If Bear found out—

"I kind of need a place to crash for a while." Meg shrugged. "I don't know how long—"

"As long as you need. Yes." Holly hugged her again and fought the anxiety rolling in her belly. "There's something I need to tell you first. Then you're welcome to change your mind if you need to."

Meg pulled back and her face pinched together. "That doesn't sound hopeful."

"We should sit and you should eat."

Without a word, Meg nodded her head and the girls fixed their plates. Holly nursed down her coffee, watching Meg eat.

"You're making me nervous, Honey." Her fork hit the plate as she set it down. "Spit it out."

Holly gripped her coffee cup and pulled her legs up in her chair, making herself as small as possible. Chills skated up her spine and not even the hot coffee chased away their cold. She closed her eyes and started spilling her guts. "First of all, please know I understand that I have handled this all wrong. I've been foolish and selfish, and instead of facing my problems, I ran. Once I started running and avoiding, it became a rhythm and I didn't know how to stop it, or… if I even wanted to."

Meg's green eyes held plenty of questions, but she simply gave one slow nod and waited for Holly to continue.

Taking a deep breath, Holly confessed her first sin. "I cheated on Lance with Justin…sort of. We were having problems, and as many times as I told Lance I wanted to break up, he never believed me or accepted it. But Justin and I were together a few times while Lance had gone off with Sean."

Meg crinkled her nose and bit her fingernail. "Okay, well, I gathered that. I mean, I had my suspicions, because you and Justin have always been…well, you and Justin. In my heart, I always knew you and Lance wouldn't last." Her disappointment was evident in the frown on her face.

While that was a small relief, it was only the beginning of this confessional. "Justin and I got married."

Meg's green eyes shot wide open and she leaned in, putting her arms on the table. "What? How did I not know that one of my best friends got married without me? When? Who the hell knows? Everyone but me?"

Holly shook her head quickly. "No one knows, or at least, no one had confirmation until last night, thanks to Justin yelling at me in the middle of a restaurant."

"Oh my God, why?"

Holly waved her hands. "I'll get there. We filed for the license, called up the preacher, grabbed Hunter and some chick he was trying to hook up with, and got married."

"When?"

"Right before Lance died." Holly's body shook, she was so nervous and frightened.

Recognition lit on Meg's face. "That's why he was angry. That's why he was drunk and on the road. He was mad at you." Her chest moved up and down with her quick breaths. "I always wondered what made him act so reckless that night."

"He wasn't just angry, Megan. He was fueled by whiskey and rage and jealousy. He…" Holly didn't want to speak the words, but if she didn't, Meg would never know the full truth. "He, um, he hit me. A couple times before that, but not nearly as severe as that night."

Meg focused in on Holly's face. "What?" She absently touched her own busted lip. "*Lance* did?"

"Hold on." In the back of Holly's dresser was a folder of pictures that the hospital had taken the night of the wreck. They showed Holly's injuries. At the time, she had lied and said all of them were from the wreck, but they weren't.

Holly gave the photos to Megan. "This cut here, he backhanded me and his class ring cut my cheek. The gash on the back of my head, the one I had to have stitches for, that was from a whiskey bottle. They had to pull the glass out and everyone assumed it was from the car. I didn't correct them. And the slash down my arm…" Holly showed her the scar she still carried that was slightly lighter than the rest of her arm. "That's where his broken bottle cut me, right before we drove off the road."

Meg stared at the pictures, as if trying to remember

back to that night. "You said they were from the wreck, from trying to get out of the car before it sank." Her voice was barely a whisper.

Holly knelt beside her. "Because I didn't want you to know, Meg. You idolized Lance and your entire family was crushed. When the paramedics called it, I knew your family couldn't handle any more horrible news. Lance was dead. What was the point in ruining your memory of him?"

"He hurt you? On more occasions than that night?" Meg's bottom lip trembled. She appeared so young, so innocent in that moment, that it took Holly right back to the night Lance died.

Holly nodded. "Never on my face. He made sure the bruises could be covered."

Meg covered her mouth with her hand and winced at her own sign of abuse. Moisture filled her eyes. "Oh, Holly. My own brother."

Holly moved to sit in the opposite chair. "That night, I went to tell Lance face-to-face that Justin and I were married, that I didn't ever want to see him again. I told him if he didn't let me go, that I would go to the police about everything he had done to me. I had pictures of all of it. Every bruise. As I turned to leave, he…he attacked me." Holly closed her eyes against the oncoming tears and tried to construct that night for Meg.

She was so scared. Lance's anger was nothing new, but never this level of crazy. He was so drunk, so angry and full of hatred for Justin and…and her. He threw the bottle first and knocked her down in the gravel driveway. With the same bottle, he knocked her over the head, shattering glass. The pain was so fierce, she nearly passed out. Blood ran through her hair, down her neck. The world started spinning, and next thing she knew, Lance had her by the collar, dragging her into his car.

Megan gasped and put both hands over her mouth, exposing only her wide, shocked eyes.

"He kept threatening me, Megan, using the broken bottle like a knife at my neck. He kept threatening to kill Justin and Hunter. I was so scared. I didn't know what to do and I started getting so dizzy. I remember rolling down the window because I couldn't concentrate. I needed to stay awake, to focus." That was when he jammed the bottle neck into her arm, thinking she was trying to get free. "Maybe I was, I don't recall. My only thought was that we were headed to Hunter and Justin's apartment and Lance kept screaming he would kill us all." By this time, Holly had tears streaming down her face and so did Meg. The worst part came next, the part where Meg would more than likely hate her forever. "I couldn't think straight. I didn't realize what I had done until the car smashed through the rails and flew through the air." Holly could still feel the way it sent her stomach into her throat like a rollercoaster.

"What are you saying?"

"I grabbed the wheel and pulled. I figured we would hit a tree or something. I didn't realize how close we were to the river."

The sedan hit hard and the impact knocked Lance out. The car flipped over before it hit the water, but she didn't know that until afterwards.

"All I focused on was getting to the surface before the car filled. Water rushed in until I couldn't breathe. My window was open and I fought to get out."

"Oh my God. You made him wreck." Meg stood and backed up. Her eyes darted around the floor and she shook her head violently, "He was drunk; the toxicology report said so."

Holly nodded. "Yes, he was extremely drunk, but that's not why he ran off the road, Megan. I'm so sorry." She didn't move, steeling herself against the oncoming storm.

Meg kept fidgeting. She kept clutching her heart, running her hands through her hair, rubbing her palms on her jeans. "He hurt you and threatened your brother and your, your, your husband. And you—"

"I killed him. I killed your bother." Holly cried as she said the words out loud. "You have every right to hate me, Meg. I hate myself."

"I don't know what I feel." She sat down and became still. "My brother had a terrible temper. I know that. He tried to hide it from me, but he was so mean to my other sister. She was older than him and they fought until the day she moved out and went to college. She barely cried at the funeral and I always wondered why."

This was news. *Lance wasn't the saint that the Smith family made him out to be?*

"I never wanted you to know what he did to me, Meg. I never wanted you to bear that burden. You're my best friend and I only wanted to protect you."

Meg silently cried for a long time. "Who else knows? Who else knows that he was abusive to you?"

Holly shook her head. "No one. Not even Hunter."

"Do you see my face, Holly?" She touched her lip and ran her fingers under her black eye. "This is what happens when you don't tell people about the monster under the bed. Lance's death might've been avoided if you had said something sooner. We could've gotten him help or counseling or something. You took those options away."

"I didn't realize what I was doing at the time, Megan, I swear. Everything happened so fast. I'm so, so sorry." Holly reached for her hand.

Green eyes met hers. "My brother is dead, Holly. Sorry doesn't cut it." Her words were soft, but Meg pulled her hand away.

"Look at what you've been through with Cole. Surely you understand."

"Thanks to the events of the last two days of my life, I completely understand being afraid of an angry, abusive man. Unlike you, the first thing I did was scream it from the rooftops because I don't want him to get away with any-thing." She framed her temples with her hands, as if trying to hold her anger in. "You buried your head in the sand. I'm not stupid, I can dissect the last six months of our lives and see how Cole's behavior escalated to this. Maybe I should've called the police on him sooner, but I didn't try to make him have a wreck or hurt himself."

"I know I didn't handle it well. I can see it now, but back then, I didn't know what to do."

"You did the typical Holly Combs act. Bury your head in the sand and pretend that all your problems go away when you don't address them. Sweep it all under the rug and call it clean. You took away our options. You made decisions that weren't yours to make." Megan's tears had turned to anger. "I'm supposed to be your best friend. How could you keep something so monumental from me, brother or not? I can't believe you didn't care enough about my feelings to let me deal with this the right way." She stormed off into the living room and started packing up her suitcase. "You're right. I don't want to stay here."

Holly followed her, grasping at her arm. "Meg, I'm

sorry. Please don't go."

"I can't—I don't want to—I need to process this and I don't want to see you right now." Meg picked up her cell and called the local cab company. It wouldn't take too long for someone to get there.

A frantic, excruciating pain came over her as Meg threw things in her bag with force. "Where will you go?"

Meg rounded on her. "As it turns out, my older sister and I have some things to discuss. Say, the real reason she left home so early. It's not that I don't believe you, I just don't…*want* to believe you. I need to talk to Laurie. I need to find out the truth about my brother. That's all there is to it."

"Megan, I never wanted to hurt you." Holly hugged herself, willing her heart and soul not to fly apart into a million pieces. Meg was her best friend and her anger was well deserved, but after last night, Holly didn't know how much more rejection and abandonment she could take.

Halting her movement, Meg tilted her head and stared at her. "I know that, Holly. I truly do. You never *mean* to hurt anyone. Your kind heart is one of your best qualities. But you've kept two life-altering secrets from me all these years and I don't even recognize you right now. Don't you think I would've celebrated you and Justin getting married, even if you weren't with my brother? Didn't you consider that I love you enough to help you through all of this? We could've supported each other."

"You left," Holly sobbed. "You were with Cole."

"That was a full year after Lance died. You lied to my face that entire year!" Meg never screamed at anyone, so her sudden outburst made Holly blanch. Meg shook her head, regaining her control. "I need to go. I can't do this right now. Laurie's house is large enough for me to stay a couple days there."

"I'm sorry."

"I know you're sorry. Now get your head out of your ass and do something about it." Meg stormed out of the house.

"You can wait inside for your ride," Holly offered, but Meg was already sitting on the front porch.

She peered over her shoulder, her green eyes full of tears. "Please leave me alone, Holly. I need a minute, okay?"

Completely deflated, Holly dropped her eyes and closed the door. She sank down, right there on the hardwood floor, and cried until she had no more tears left to cry. It amplified when she heard the door of the cab slam and the fading crunch of tires on the rock driveway.

If she lay there and died of a broken heart, would anyone but Hunter even care?

JUSTIN ROLLED OVER TO ANSWER HIS RINGING CELL phone. He didn't recognize the number. For a split second, he considered sending it to voicemail. Despite his run into the early hours of the morning, he hadn't slept well. A little voice told him not to ignore the call. "Yeah, hello?"

"Justin? It's Megan."

"Red-headed, short-shit Megan?"

A high-pitched, sweet chuckle on the other end. "Yes, red-headed, short-shit Megan." That had been his nickname for her for years.

"Well, well, well, to what do I owe the pleasure? How's the weather in Boston?"

"I'm not in Boston. I'm in Dalton."

Justin sat up. *Did Bear know?* "That's great. We would all love to see you—"

"No," she spat out quickly. "Um, please don't tell anyone I'm here. It's been a rough couple of days and I'm headed to stay with my sister for a while. The reason I'm calling isn't about me. It's Holly."

"What's wrong?" Justin languidly sat on the edge of his bed.

"She's not well, Justin."

That got his full attention. "What do you mean? What's going on?"

"I went to her house last night. We talked. I know the truth. I know you're married."

"She told you?" *Holy crap. That's huge.*

"Do you still love her? Do you still want to be married to her?"

His heart lurched in his chest. Holly told her about their marriage? Either Holly had accepted the fact that they were married…or accepted the fact that they were getting divorced. The idea of a life without Holly was akin to no life at all. Over the last few months, he had tried to accept the fact his life might have to be dull in her absence. But he didn't want to live a shadow of what could've been. "Of course I do, Megan. I always have, I always will."

"I figured." There was a smile in her voice.

"That doesn't mean I'm willing to let her keep ripping my heart out. I don't know how much more I can take."

"She needs you, Justin. Now."

As soon as he heard those words, he reached for his pants and shoes while Meg kept talking.

"She told me why she left. Everything. And you wouldn't believe the secrets she has kept. You need to make her talk, Justin. You might be able to save your marriage. Don't wait. I walked out on her this morning and I know she's sorry," Meg choked up and it took her a moment to compose her thoughts. "She's broken, Justin. She's broken in a way only you and God can fix."

Fifteen minutes later, Justin was on the road headed to Dalton. He didn't know what to expect. He had two things with him: the wedding rings they had ordered before the accident and the divorce papers. At this point, he could flip a coin and have a better chance of determining the outcome. He dared not wait, though. He wouldn't leave it to Holly's discretion any longer.

Driving up the gravel road leading to Holly's family cabin in the woods amped up his nerves. How many times had they came here as teenagers for weekend getaways? It was full of memories. Great memories. Most of his memories with Holly were great—up until Lance ruined it all. Hate might be a strong word, and his mama preached about not hating people and forgiveness and all the things he remembered from church. However, if he was capable of hating someone, Lance Smith came damn close.

With each creaking stair to the porch, his confidence wavered. He knocked and said a little prayer.

His heart shuddered when Holly answered the door in nothing but cotton shorts and a tank top. "Justin." Her eyes were red and puffy, her nose was pink, and her bottom lip trembled. She was still his lovely wife.

"Meg called." The mention of Meg made Holly burst into tears. To his utter shock, Holly threw her arms around his neck and collapsed against him. "Hey, wow, okay. Let's go inside, babe." He ushered her to the couch and held her while she cried. She felt so right in his arms, even in her pain. It was only natural to hold her and love her. He didn't know any other reaction to Holly, even against his better judgment at times.

"What happened?" He stroked her hair, loving the smell and softness of it.

"She hates me, Justin. My best friend hates me and I don't know if she can ever forgive me for what I did."

"What did you do? Talk to me, Holly. For once, will you please be honest with me? Trust me enough to know the truth. We can get through this." Based on the way she clung to him now, he took a chance and assumed that they were far from over. He reached out and took her hand in his. "I'm done with this separation, Honey. You're my girl. You have been since we were in grade school."

Tears overflowed and Holly clamped her eyes shut. "You don't want me, Justin. Not now. I'm not that girl you married by the river."

Running his fingers over her cheek, he wiped her tears. "Then who are you? Show me. Give me the chance to make up my own mind. I deserve that."

Holly shook her head, pushed away, and stood. She wrung out her hands and paced in front of the windows of her cabin. Every breath came as a struggle. Was she having a panic attack? Did he need to get her some water or something?

Holly blurted out, "I killed him."

That ceased all inner ramblings. Justin's brows dipped low. "Who?"

"Lance. I killed him."

Justin straightened on the couch and leaned his elbows on his knees. Surely he hadn't heard that right. Holly was one of the gentlest souls on the planet. "Holly, what are you talking about? Lance died in a drunk driving accident."

She swayed back and forth, hugging herself. They had

been through a lot and yet he had never seen her this upset, this unsettled, and off balance emotionally.

"What happened the night of the accident, Holly?"

Fresh tears covered her cheeks and she wiped them away. "I went to his house, you know, to just tell him everything, make sure he knew beyond the shadow of a doubt that we were done and that I loved you. I told him about us, about our marriage, and that I was done with his abuse—"

"Abuse?" Justin was on his feet in a blink. "What abuse?" Anger raged in his mind, but he kept his voice calm.

Holly still flinched, and she stepped away from him. "I should've told you. I'm sorry. Megan was completely right." She pushed her hair out of her face with both hands. "If I had spoken up earlier, if I had said something the first time he laid a hand on me, none of this would've happened."

"Jesus, Holly." He held her shoulders. "He hit you?"

She clamped her eyes closed and nodded, her lip trembling again.

Everything made sense now. Pieces of the puzzle that had been missing for four years now fell into place. A picture of the truth formed in his mind. *If that asshole wasn't already dead…*

"Keep going, Honey. I've got you now."

"He was already drinking whiskey and started pushing me around, yelling at me, calling me a whore. I tried to stand up to him, but when I turned to leave, he threw a bottle at my head. It scared me. I honestly don't remember if I fell or if I ducked, but he picked up the bottle and hit me, broke it against my head. I have pictures—"

"I remember." Vividly. Seeing Holly covered in blood, passed out in the hospital, had taken ten years off his life. Justin ran his hands up her arms, touching the faded scar on her arm from the broken bottle. "You said this was from the accident."

Holly shook her head. "I didn't want anyone to know. Meg thought Lance hung the moon and stars. She was so upset when he died. I couldn't do that to her, her parents, our friends."

"God, Holly. You should've told me." He kept her cradled in his arms. Holly melted into him, his body craving her affection more than his next breath. Justin rubbed at the base of her neck, something he had done since they were in high school. It always made her feel better. "Tell me what happened next."

Holly nodded against his shoulder and took a steadying breath. "We fought and argued and he kept throwing things at me. There was so much blood and I tried to run, but he caught me and picked me up and shoved me into his car. He told me that if I resisted, he would kill me. At that moment, I truly believed he would. He was so mad. He wanted you dead, Justin. The moment I realized we were heading to the apartment you and Hunter shared, I… I didn't think…I grabbed the wheel and the car went sailing. The moment we hit the water, he went unconscious. There was blood on the window. I assumed he hit his head." Holly stepped out of Justin's arms to see that he had red rings around his eyes. She touched his face. "If he had hurt you—"

Justin grabbed her wrists but kept her hands on his face. "Damn it, Holly. You nearly *died!*" He leaned his forehead to hers. "You should've let him come. Hunter and I would've handled him."

"I'd never seen him so angry, so insane with jealousy. It scared me. And I was so afraid Meg would see him." Holly pushed him back, dark shadows in her eyes. "I couldn't bring myself to tell Meg, but I…I let him drown. I looked back. I could've gotten to him before the car filled. I could've got him out. But I…I didn't even try. After everything he put me through, I didn't care. I swam hard to the shore and watched the car disappear." Holly covered her mouth with the back of her hand. "I watched him sink, knowing that he would die. Knowing what everyone would lose, knowing Megan and their family would be distraught, knowing his friends would miss him. I didn't care. He hurt me so much and I didn't care." Holly bawled on his shoulder. With every breath, she cried, "I'm sorry. I killed him and I'm so sorry."

"Shh. It's okay, Honey. It's over now." How had she carried this guilt all these years?

Everything made sense now. Holly hadn't been avoiding him and their marriage all this time. She was suffering from severe post-traumatic stress and one of the ways she handled it was to avoid everything that reminded her of the night Lance died.

What a self-centered fool he'd been.

He held her close and walked her to the bathroom. He wet a rag and wiped her face. Even without makeup, Holly Combs was the most astoundingly gorgeous woman he'd ever seen. She would often forgo makeup, as if that would somehow hide her beauty. As if ponytails and baseball caps could hide the unique golden honey color of her hair or the sparkle in her sky-blue eyes. Even with nothing but Chapstick, her lips attracted the eyes of every man around. The few mornings he was blessed to wake up beside her, Justin would watch her sleep and wonder how the devil he landed such a woman.

Unlike most men, he loved her for more than her beauty. He and Holly shared a passion for fast cars, spending lazy weekends on the river or out in nature. They used to fish together, hike together, hunt together. She used to be his best friend. Man, he missed that.

"Why are you staring at me like that?" she asked between hiccups as she caught her breath.

"I can't believe you've lived with this secret all these years. All this time, I assumed you didn't love me. I've missed you, Honey. You're my best friend, or, we *used* to be best friends. I wish you would've trusted me with this." He ran his hand over her cheek. "There's nothing that would make me stop loving you. We should've dealt with this *together*. That's what married people do."

"Please don't divorce me." Holly's red-rimmed eyes pleaded with him. She grabbed on to his shirt in desperation. "I'll get my shit together, I swear."

His shoulders fell. "Holly." He sighed and wrapped his arms around her again. "I'm not going anywhere."

Holly clung to him so tightly, he couldn't breathe. It didn't matter. His woman was in his arms again and he wasn't ever letting her go. Meg was right. Holly's guilt had broken her and she needed love more than anything right now. He didn't fault Meg for needing some space. She'd recently learned a frightening truth about her brother and that would be difficult on anyone. But there was no way Justin could turn his back on Holly now. In a life or death moment, she made choices no one should have to make. He wouldn't leave her alone to deal with those demons any longer.

She finally cried herself out and slowly released her vise grip. "Sorry. I can't seem to control the waterworks." She wiped her wet cheeks. "I haven't cried so much in years."

"It's okay. I'll hold you for as long as you need me to."

"Promise?"

That innocent vulnerability in her eyes twisted his heart. She needed him, always had, and she simply didn't know it.

Justin cupped her cheeks and met her eyes. "Listen to me, Honey. When I vowed to love you until death do us part, I meant it. Yes, I'm going to take you over my knee for waiting this long to tell me, but I never stopped loving you. No matter what I tried."

"You said you were filing—"

"I was jealous. That's all." He kissed her forehead. "Turns out I don't enjoy seeing my wife on dates with other men. Crazy. I know."

They both chuckled and stared at each other for a moment before Holly's eyes dropped and she pushed her hair behind her ears. She picked up his hand and examined his fingernails. No matter what he did, he couldn't seem to get them completely free from the evidence of his job.

"Grease monkey." Holly kissed his knuckles.

"Job hazard."

Her sad smile stung him right in the heart. "What do I do, Justin? Meg knows what happened, but I didn't tell her there was a chance I could've gotten Lance out. She's so angry with me now, I can't imagine what she'll do—"

He gripped her shoulder. "Listen to me, Holly. The hard truth is, Lance was a prick and now he's a dead prick. Hunter and I never understood what Bear and Chris saw in him. Sean was his weed-smoking partner, but still. He and I nearly came to blows several times over the years and that was before he went after you.

"Realistically, you probably would've both died if you had tried to save him. You're not a great swimmer anyway.

So, for the love of God, get that idea out of your head. You could *not* have pulled his unconscious body out of that car, especially since it was upside down and rapidly filling with water. You're lucky you made it out alive, as crazy as the river is in that region. Let that go. Yes, you made a mistake by grabbing the wheel, but you weren't thinking straight. You had a concussion. The EMTs confirmed it. You had to think twice when they asked your name. Unless people have been in a life-or-death situation, they can't criticize your actions. It's over. It's done. You can't take it back and you damn sure can't live your entire life in isolation."

"You don't hate me?" she asked with obvious doubt and surprise.

"Never. You almost died trying to protect me. Hell, at this point, I love you more."

"Meg hates me."

"If Megan hated you, she wouldn't have called me to come comfort you. You added salt to a fresh wound because she's dealing with her own crap. Give her time."

Holly nodded and sniffed. "Do you guess everyone else will be angry too?"

Justin shrugged. "I can't answer that. But I can tell you this for sure: Tina, Jayden, Keri; they miss you fiercely. They don't need to know the gory details. Tell them the basics. We got married, Lance found out and was threatening you, coming after me, you two fought before the car went into the river and you've always blamed yourself for making him angry enough to be reckless. That's it. That's enough."

Holly nodded and seemed to be calming down. "Okay. You're right. I don't have to go into great details. Meg probably wouldn't want me to anyhow."

Even in that moment, she still thought about protecting Meg more than herself. That was part of the reason he loved her. Her self-sacrifice was a double-edged sword.

"Where does all this leave us?" Holly hugged herself again.

Justin tilted her chin up with his fingers. He didn't say anything; he simply kissed her softly and slowly, trying to convey his unending love for her. It took her a moment, but Holly's hands slowly trailed up his chest and around his neck. The chill from all the death talk dissipated as their kiss warmed him from head to toe. He leaned his forehead against hers.

"I love you, Holly. Nothing will change that. I'm sorry for what I said last night in the restaurant. I didn't mean it."

"I hope not. I was so upset about that, I lost half a bottle of rum in the river. I won't mention how I fell in before the bottle did." She rolled her eyes.

He remembered finding the bottle when he went out for a run. "That's so weird. I was at the park, on the jogging trail, and I found a half empty bottle of Captain Morgan. It reminded me of you because the label was torn around the edges."

Holly's eyes went wide. "No way! You found my rum? When was this? It would've taken hours to get downstream that far."

Justin rubbed the back of his neck. "It was about three this morning. I couldn't sleep. My mind was on you."

"That's…that's so crazy. Like the river carried it to you." Holly shook her head. "Funny, I always kind of thought the river kept us apart."

"Me too. But now I realize it connected us. It gave me a reminder of you. I know I was a jerk that night, and I yelled and threatened divorce, but that's not at all what I want."

"What *do* you want?"

"You." He ran his fingers over her cheek. "The rest of that bottle of rum." They both grinned. Holly's eyes sparked with the first sign of hope he had seen in a long time. "I want the life we talked about. My incredibly sexy wife. I want to have a family with you. Girls with your sweet smile and talent for art. Boys with my knack for cars and perpetually dirty fingernails. A home full of 'em. Dogs, maybe. I know you don't care for animals that much, but I believe I can persuade you…eventually."

Holly chuckled, then her brows furrowed. "What about a really ugly cat?"

"Huh? Oh, yeah." He glanced around, seeking the feline. "I guess, sure."

Holly pointed to her bed, where a ball of brown fur stared at them.

"Oh my God! That cat is fugly."

Holly slapped his chest. They walked into the bedroom and he picked up the cat, looking it in the face—at least he hoped that was a face. "No, for real, this cat is effin' ugly."

About that time, it let out one zombie screech and pawed at Justin's face.

Holly laughed when Justin flinched and frowned, his nose crinkling up. "Don't make fun of Arby. He's sensitive."

"Arby?" Justin set down the cat and perched on the edge of the bed. "You named him after a roast beef sandwich?"

"Arby, as in the letter R and the letter B. Stands for Rat Bastard."

Justin coughed and chuckled. "You named him Rat

Bastard, but I can't call him ugly because it would hurt his little kitty feelings? Talk about your double standards."

"Exactly. Only I can make fun because I have to live with it, *him*, whatever."

Justin rolled his eyes. "Fine, but I want a badass dog. We're going to have to balance out the scales if we keep this guy."

Holly nodded and took a deep breath. "Can you stay? Today and maybe…tonight? Or do you have to go home?"

"I'll stay." Hell yeah, he was staying. After four of the most miserable years of his life, Holly wanted to spend time with him. It was all he dreamed about for the last few years. "Please tell me you have beer."

They popped the top on a couple beers and Justin made small talk while Holly gathered herself. She made them lunch, simply to keep herself busy. He told her all about how Bo and Tina came to be a couple, how he became close friends with Bo, and caught her up on all the things she'd missed.

Hours later, Holly had her head in his lap, prattling on about her dreaded job at the bank, the Barracuda, and the life she'd tried to create here in Dalton. The weird cat had curled up on her stomach and purred as it rested. She'd never been into animals, so to see her petting and loving on a cat was new.

It amazed him how, after all this time, they conversed and talked the same way they'd done since they were children. Sure, there were some differences now. There was a longing in her voice when she asked about their hometown and their friends. At the same time, she seemed content here. They sat out on the pier for a couple hours and tinkered with the 'Cuda for the rest of the afternoon until dinner. Then ordered take-out and curled up on the couch.

"Holly, I have something I want you to do, while we're working on us and moving forward." Justin swallowed hard.

That vulnerable expression came back to her eyes. "What?"

"I want you to talk to someone. A therapist or someone who deals with PTSD."

She dropped her eyes and played with her fork and the box she held for a moment. "That's probably a good idea."

Justin reached out and rubbed her leg. "Sean actually suggested it. He's seeing someone too." He didn't like the way she frowned. "Baby, you need to deal with the guilt and the trauma. I can't give you the kind of counseling you need. But I promise to love you through it. I'll be right with you, every step of the way."

Holly's lips pinched together in a thin smile and she nodded.

When they both yawned in sync, Justin grinned. "Guess it's time to hit the hay. If you have an extra blanket, I'll take the couch."

Holly sat up and held out a hand. "I think my husband can sleep in the same bed as me." Once again, he read the trepidation in her eyes. Holly expected his rejection at every turn. Only time would take that fear away.

As nice as sleeping in the same bed sounded, he wasn't about to assume anything. Four years was a long time to live separated from the one you loved. It did things to a person's brain. Mainly the brain below his belt. "Holly, we don't have to pretend this is a normal marriage. We can start fresh, take things slow. We can work this thing out in our own time."

She flinched and withdrew her hand a couple inches. "Right. Of course. Silly me."

Grabbing her hand before she retreated further, he pulled her down into his lap. Much to his surprise, Holly straddled him. His heartbeat rocketed and he sucked in a breath. "Baby, I haven't held you or kissed you or touched your body in so long, I'm afraid what I might do given that opportunity. Do you have any idea how many nights I've laid in bed dreaming of you? Remembering the way we made love and played in bed?"

"Probably as many nights as I have." She cupped his face and brought her lips within a hairline of his. "Are you trying to tell me you don't want to kiss me, or hold me, or wake up next to me?"

Damn, do I ever.

Her whispered words tickled his lips and called every nerve in his body to attention. Each deep breath brought her scent into his lungs. Justin slid his hands up her thighs and caressed her bottom. The seduction in her eyes heated his blood like no other woman on earth. The way her thighs cradled his waist, she couldn't possibly miss his growing arousal.

Denying Holly had always been impossible. The moment their bodies touched or his lips met hers, fire ignited. He remembered all too well how it felt to make love to her. Those memories had kept him warm on many lonely nights. For years, he prayed he would have this chance again, and now that it was here, he didn't want to pass it up.

However, there couldn't be any secrets between them, especially not about sex.

With his eyes clenched shut, he said the one thing that might stop her advances. "I, um, need to tell you something. There was this girl, about a year or so back. It was one night, we were both drunk, but we, um—"

Holly covered his mouth with the tips of her fingers. "And I had dates less than a week ago. No sex, but I was considering it. How about we not try to sabotage this, okay? I've done that enough for the both of us. From this moment forward, it's me and you, babe. Nothing else matters. I'm your wife; you're my husband, and…I love you."

Happiness bloomed in his chest and all the air rushed from his lungs. "Yeah." He choked up. "Sounds like a perfect plan." He buried his hands in her soft hair. "I love you too, Honey."

Fresh tears glistened in her eyes. "Yeah?"

"Always have, always will."

Holly mirrored his smile and nuzzled her nose to his. Their lips met and the embers that sat waiting all this time flamed up in a deluge of desire. Justin buried his hands in her long hair and angled her head to deepen their kiss. The sweetest moan escaped her lips and she wiggled closer.

He wasted no time discarding her shirt, making the cat yowl when he accidentally threw it on him.

Holly giggled and unbuttoned his first few buttons. "Don't mind him, he's cranky."

"Me or the cat?" Justin laughed and stood with her in his arms.

She snorted and hugged his neck tight as he took her into the bedroom.

"I've been without you for four years, woman." Justin tossed her on the bed.

"That would make any man cranky." Holly leaned up on her elbows and bit her bottom lip.

Justin pulled his shirt off and grinned down at her.

"I plan on waking up with a smile on my face tomorrow, baby."

With a devilish twinkle in her eye, Holly looped her finger through his belt and tugged him on top of her. "Why don't I help you with that?"

The next morning, Holly stretched, loving the feeling of soft sheets on her naked skin and the dull ache between her thighs. Justin lay tucked close behind her, one hand on her breast, one leg thrown over her hip.

"Mmm. I knew I'd wake up with a smile." He nuzzled his nose to her neck.

"G'morning, Mr. Meyers," Holly said with a smile of her own.

"Good morning, *Mrs.* Meyers."

Holy shit. Holly froze and then rolled over to meet his eyes. "Mrs. Meyers?" She swallowed hard. "That's going to be an adjustment."

Justin casually shrugged a shoulder and yawned his next words. "You don't have to take my last name. I'm not worried about the details." He cupped her bottom and pulled her close, intertwining their legs.

"Shouldn't we worry about a few details? What being a real married couple is going to be like? How we'll tell our friends, our family?"

Justin narrowed his eyes and quirked his lips to the side. "Hmm. Okay, let's start with the easy one: telling people. My parents sort of already know. So that's done."

"What?" Holly jerked up on her elbow and stared wide-eyed at him.

"My mom and step-dad were starting to wonder why I didn't date. They kept trying to fix me up, even asked if I was gay. I had to tell them so they would leave me alone."

"Oh." Her brows furrowed. "Do you think us being back together will make them upset?" How would his parents feel about her abandoning their son for all this time?

"I don't care. I have my wife naked in my arms. Screw the rest of the world. I'm happier than I have been in years."

About then, a clap of thunder shook the cabin. Holly rolled over to peek out the window. "Ooh, we can go watch it rain. Come on. There's nothing better than watching the rain dance on the river."

"Can we stay naked? I'm still getting used to this view." He groped her bottom again.

"Bring a blanket, Captain Grab-ass. I'll start the coffee."

A few minutes later, they cuddled under a soft blanket with two cups of coffee sending wisps of steam into the rain-cooled morning air.

"Can I ask you something?" Justin took a sip of his black coffee.

That question never ended well for her, but she nodded anyway.

"Are you ashamed to be married to me?"

"No!" Holly ran a hand up his chest to his neck. "Heavens no. What makes you say that?"

He shrugged a shoulder. "I was just wondering. I remember your mama calling me a charming but low-class grease head that wouldn't amount to anything."

"Sounds like my mother, dear Lord." Holly rolled her eyes and groaned. She drank her coffee and settled into his arms. "My mother doesn't live in this version of reality. She's still stuck in 1980s Hollywood reality."

Justin chuckled.

"Mom thinks Hunter and I waste our looks. She warns us all the time that life won't be so kind to us after our beauty fades and time takes its toll." She imitated her mother's melodramatic tone. "Life hasn't been too kind, even with our attractiveness."

Holly and Hunter's mother had graced the silver screen in the seventies and eighties. She'd never landed a major role but often played the sexy, distracting female that lured men into bed. Unfortunately, she'd adopted that role in real-life.

Justin gently kissed her temple. "You're exceedingly beautiful, Honey. But you're also pretty damn amazing. People are missing out on the best part of you if they don't dig deeper."

Holly's insides fluttered and a silly grin spread across her face. "You're still the one person who can call me beautiful and I feel something besides nausea."

His brown eyebrows dipped. "You weren't always that way. What happened? Lance?"

If only Lance were the sole source of her bitterness. Between her pretty face, blond hair, and generous curves, no one had ever taken her seriously. No one, save her closest friends, had ever treated her as more than a blond bimbo. During her modeling days, men and women alike harassed her. As if being attractive somehow equated to being easy. Even the bank where she worked kept her in a visual position at the teller-window because customers liked seeing her face. She'd been passed over twice for promotions that she deserved. Ladies would joke over the lunch table that she must live a charmed life.

If they only knew the half of it.

"Not only him. But he furthered it along more than most."

His lips brushed her temple again and again. "I'm sorry, Holly. For everything. For Lance hurting you and not coming to get you sooner. I waited because I thought that's what you needed."

"I did, Justin. Maybe not this long, but I needed time. I shouldn't have been such a coward. Megan needed to know about Lance years ago; you all did. But I was too scared to admit the truth. Now that I have, I'm afraid I've lost her." Holly's voice caught and she fought back tears. Megan was her best friend in high school and the possibility of losing her ripped Holly apart.

"Well, this is going to make Tina's wedding interesting. Meg is one of her bridesmaids too, right?"

She nodded. "Meg would never cause a scene at Tina's wedding. Neither of us would ruin it for T."

"You have a few months before the event. I'm sure after a while, you can call and talk to her. She needs time too." Justin kept up his sweet kisses to her temple and moved to her ear.

His lips sent chills racing across her skin. He still

remembered the places that made her melt.

"You need to give your two weeks' notice at work," he whispered.

That was a change of subject that zapped her out of a trance. "Huh?"

"Well, you aren't going to remain here, right? Traditionally, husbands and wives share homes. It's time, Honeycomb, time to come back to Riverview, to the people who love and miss you."

Holly swallowed hard. "I do miss getting to see my friends."

"What about your perfect twin brother?" Holly and Justin jumped clear out of their skin when Hunter came sauntering around the edge of the house and stopped dead in his tracks upon seeing their current state. "Oh my God, are y'all naked?" Hunter covered his eyes. "Dear Lord!"

"What're you doing here?" Holly grabbed as much of the blanket as Justin could spare and covered her body.

Hunter kept his eyes covered and chuckled. "Your text said to come over this morning. Obviously, I'm early."

"I didn't invite you."

Justin cleared his throat. "Um, I did."

"What the—" Holly yanked the blanket away from Justin, leaving him completely uncovered.

"Oops. Don't look, Hunt!" He laughed and covered his junk as he ran back in the cabin.

Hunter brayed with laughter as Holly wrapped herself up. "I'm assuming you two made up?"

"You know what they say about assuming," Holly growled.

"I *am* seeing a lot of ass right now."

Brothers. Ugh.

Holly stomped back in the house and to her bedroom, where Justin had slid on some shorts. "Why did you text him?" she growled in a whisper.

"He deserves to know, Holly. He's your twin and my best friend. No one loves you more than he does, save maybe me." Justin grabbed the blanket and pulled her close to his chest. "No more secrets, okay? I love you."

She arched a brow, her aggravation not totally gone. She couldn't deny him affection, not after everything they'd been through. "I love you too, brat."

"Grease monkey." Hunter rapped on the bedroom door. "You better not be making out with my sister in there."

"If making out offends him, thank goodness he doesn't know what all I kissed last night." Justin grinned and dipped his head to rub his nose against hers as she gasped.

A while later, Holly's knee bounced nervously as she sat on the couch next to Justin, facing her brother. She gave Hunter the short and not-so-sweet version of what happened.

"I'm tired of running, Hunter." Holly wiped a single tear from her cheek.

Justin squeezed her hand gently. "And we both want this marriage to work. That starts with dealing with some demons."

Hunter's nostrils flared and he muttered *sonofabitch* under his breath. His chest rose and fell with heavy breaths. "You didn't say anything back then. You never told me about Lance."

"I never told anyone."

"But I'm your brother," he yelled and jumped to his feet. "I am your twin, for shit's sake! We're supposed to share things, *everything*." Emotion welled up and his eyes misted over. "I would've protected you! I should've known."

Holly's own emotions and guilt had her eyes watering. "I was afraid no one would believe me. Everyone loved Lance. He had this perfect, charming façade and no one wanted to see anything but how great he was. After he died, his family, Megan, they all talked about him like he was a saint. Meg was so upset; I couldn't tell her. I couldn't ruin that memory for her…for any of you."

"Maybe I didn't show it very well, but I was not a fan of Lance Smith. I tolerated him because of everyone else and for your sake. I would've happily kicked his ass ten ways to Sunday, *especially* if I had known he hurt my sister. What were you thinking?"

"I was thinking people would go insane, exactly how you are now."

"So you ran away? Like a coward? Typical Holly, sweep it under the rug and hope no one sees the truth."

Holly's mouth hung open. Was that what he thought about her?

"Hey." Justin rose to her defense. "You don't know what she went through. None of us do. She nearly died that night because Lance was threatening us. Don't ever call her a coward. She's facing it right now in the best way she knows how."

Hunter put his hands on his hips, closed his eyes, and took a deep breath. "What if I had lost you, Holly?"

"At that moment, I didn't care if I died…as long as he didn't hurt the people I love. I was afraid of him. Don't you understand?"

Hunter's anger deflated like a burst balloon. He pulled her up and hugged her tight. "I'm sorry, Honey. God, I'm so damn sorry."

"It's not your fault. I never spoke up. It's my fault." Holly loved the security she found in her brother. Finally, after four of the most miserable years of her life, she openly wept to her family about the trauma she'd suffered.

Hunter apologized repeatedly, petting her hair and rubbing her back. "Please, please don't keep secrets from me, Holly. You're my sister, my twin. There's nothing I wouldn't do for you. I never would've put my friendship with anyone above my sister. It's my responsibility to protect you."

Holly pulled back slightly and wiped the tears from her eyes. Man, she loved her brother, and she hated herself for not trusting him with the truth all this time. She'd figured if no one learned the truth, it could never hurt anyone.

She was wrong.

"I think, technically, it's my responsibility to protect you, since I'm the older twin." She grinned through her tears.

Hunter rolled his eyes. "Not even. I'm taller, which makes you my *little* sister."

Justin groaned from the couch, "Dear God, not this argument again." Sitting in his lap, happily purring, was Arby. "Some things never change, Arby."

"Ugh, what the hell are you holding?" Hunter wrinkled up his nose, making his otherwise perfect face turn sour. He kept an arm looped around Holly's shoulders.

"This is the other man who's been sleeping with my wife." Justin picked Arby up and examined him. "At least she didn't get someone hotter."

"You know what they say about animals resembling their owners. You're well on your way with that one. Ugly sonofabitch." Hunter chuckled.

"Ha ha." Justin shot him the bird. "I bagged your sister

last night. *Twice.* How'd you like them apples?"

"Justin!" Holly covered her face with her hands and felt the blazing heat of embarrassment engulf her skin.

Hunter pulled his arm back slowly. "Gross. Married or not, *so* gross."

The three of them laughed and a comfortable peace fell over Holly for the first time in years. The two men who meant the most to her finally knew her secrets and still loved her despite her sins.

Tʜᴇ ɴᴇxᴛ ꜰᴇᴡ ᴡᴇᴇᴋs ᴘʀᴏᴠᴇᴅ ᴛʜᴇ ʜᴀʀᴅᴇsᴛ ᴀɴᴅ ʏᴇᴛ the most fulfilling weeks of Holly's life. Their family and friends were less than pleased that Holly and Justin had kept secrets from them. They were completely taken off guard by the marriage, and shockingly *un*surprised by the revelation of Lance's abuse. As it turned out, Lance hadn't fooled people nearly as efficiently as Holly assumed. While they all mourned his passing, it was more for Meg's benefit.

Jayden confided that once, knowing she was married to Christopher, Lance had propositioned her and didn't take her rejection well. Tina believed that Lance and Holly had been engaged at one point because Lance spread that rumor. Sean reluctantly opened up about some of the things he had witnessed Lance do while they were drunk or high. It was no shock to him to hear that Holly had been abused. Bear had a harder time believing Lance would hurt anyone, but he often focused on the best in people. Now that multiple stories of Lance's poor character surfaced, they each wished they had been the one to speak up sooner.

It all added up to one simple truth. All this time, Holly had been so worried about soiling Lance's memory, but he had done plenty while he was alive to soil it himself. If she had only come clean right when things went south, she would've had all the support she needed to protect herself.

Her parents were livid about her being married. Sitting in front of her mother, step-dad, father, and step-mom and letting them in on her huge secret had been difficult. Her strength came from Justin. No matter who she faced, no matter what their reaction was, Justin held her hand and supported her. He was her champion and her defender. Only because of him did she have the courage to change her situation.

The day she left the First Bank of Dalton, her co-workers threw her a party. Leaving a job had never felt better. Holly had applied at the gallery in Riverview and finally had a chance to put her art degree to work.

Moving in with Justin was a transition. Nearly four years of living in a picturesque, secluded, river-side cabin made her spoiled. The tiny two-bedroom apartment close to downtown wasn't ideal. However, she could walk to work. Coming home to Justin every night made up for it. They fixed the 'Cuda, they went fishing, they jogged together in the mornings, and made love at night. She had her best friend back and it changed her entire outlook. Her life was finally that…a life.

Holly, with her family's blessing, offered the Dalton cabin, rent free, to Meg. Their first step to reconciliation.

"And I'm seeing a therapist once a week," Holly told

Tina as they drove the Barracuda to Dalton early that Saturday morning for a girls' weekend at the cabin. The second step to reconciliation with Meg. "It's uncomfortable as a root canal, but I haven't had a panic attack in three weeks. I'm finally living again, you know?"

"I get it and I'm so friggin' thankful. God, I was seriously about to invade your life—"

"With power tools?" Holly laughed when Tina narrowed her eyes at her.

"Power tools, nail guns, whatever it took to get you to come home."

Holly visualized Tina busting into her cabin, her tool belt stocked and a nail gun in each hand, a cowboy ready for a showdown. She giggled to herself.

They were quiet for a spell, enjoying the rumbling of the engine and the drive up the road that followed the river. The heavy rains in May had the water flowing high in June.

"I, um, I know I've been a pain in the ass, but thanks for never giving up on me, Tina. No one gave up on me, but you pushed me harder than the others. I'm glad you did."

Tina smiled, softening the angles of her face. "You're our Honeycomb. Life wouldn't be as *sweet* without you."

Holly reached over and took Tina's hand. "Thanks."

"Eh, save it for Justin. No matter how bad things got, he always had faith that you would come back to us."

Her heart kicked up a couple beats at the mention of his name. Their love had grown and flourished since they moved in together and were working on their marriage. Not to say it wasn't challenging; she was quite tired of NASCAR. At the end of the day, all he had to do was kiss her and they went up in flames, enjoying a passion for each other that had been there since high school. Justin enabled her to tap into happiness she had feared far gone from her heart.

"I can't believe I get to spend the rest of my life with him." Holly shook her head and sighed, smiling because she couldn't *not* smile when she thought about Justin and what their future might be like.

"I know exactly what you mean. That's how I feel every time I see Bo. And now we're planning a wedding and I'm so inept at these kinds of things. I'm thrilled that you and Jayden are helping."

"I'm happy to," Holly said, genuinely excited to be a part of Tina's life again. "Justin and I didn't exactly have a formal ceremony, so I'm totally living vicariously through you." It had been so much fun going shopping with the girls, picking out their bridesmaids' dresses, shoes, admiring floral arrangements, reminders that life is full of color and joy if you only embrace it.

They turned down the long driveway leading to the cabin.

There were cars everywhere.

"What the heck?" Holly carefully maneuvered through two vans, a caterer, and a florist.

"I'm really glad you've been helping me plan my wedding," Tina said absently, craning her neck to examine the logos on the vans. "It made it easier to plan yours." She gave Holly a devilish grin and wiggled her eyebrows.

"What!" Holly screeched.

Tina's laughter filled the car. "You're getting *married*! Well, remarried!"

The world spun, but this time, it wasn't a panic attack. It was pure excitement and joy that Holly couldn't contain. "You're kidding me."

"Nope!" Tina clapped her hands. "I'm not ready to pick out my wedding crap yet. All the shopping last week was for you."

"Tina!" Holly parked the car in front of her family's cabin and wiped the tears streaming down her face.

"Not just me. Jayden, Keri, Meg, your mom, your step-mom; we all conspired to pull this off."

On cue, women spilled out of the cabin in matching sage green robes. There was her mother, her step-mom, two of her cousins, one of her aunts, and her best friends.

Holly was so overcome, she sat there and cried tears of joy until Tina came to the driver's side door and helped her out.

"Dear thing I haven't done my makeup." Jayden swiped at the tears on her face.

Holly hugged them all and laughed. Until she came to Megan. The two ladies stared at each other.

"Tina and I fought over who would be the maid of honor. I told her I didn't care how many nail guns or staplers she had." She wiped the moisture from her face and her chin trembled. "You're my best friend, damn it. And they kind of invaded my house." She pointed over her shoulder to the cabin that was slowly transforming into a wedding venue.

Holly yanked Meg into her arms and held on for dear life. Meg hugged her back as hard. They had a lot to talk about, but that would come later.

The ladies ushered Holly into the bedroom of the cabin, where a wedding dress hung in the corner. It was one that she had modeled for a bridal shop in Dalton about a year ago. Holly clamped her hands over her mouth. In her opinion, it was the perfect dress for her bust size and hips.

"How did you know?" she whispered to the group of ladies standing behind her.

Her mother came forward and hugged her from behind. "You told me that you loved this dress because it made you feel like a princess. I called the shop and asked if they still had one in your size. The owner was pleased to know his favorite model would wear her favorite dress from his collection…for a small rental fee." She rolled her eyes and smiled. "Happy wedding day, baby girl."

The A-line dress had lace applique sleeves and a deep V-neck that accentuated her curves. The wide, princess-style skirt was layers of tulle and a lace applique overlay that trailed behind her.

Her dream dress for her dream husband.

"I need Justin," Holly whispered, then cleared her throat and faced her friends. "I need to talk to him."

"The groom isn't supposed to see you on the wedding day." Tina's brow arched.

Holly huffed. "Justin and I kissed tradition and rules goodbye long ago."

Everyone laughed and Tina ran off to get Justin. A moment later, he stood outside the door, careful not to peek inside the room.

"Can we have a moment?" The room cleared at Holly's request. She stayed in the room and Justin on the other side of the door.

"Are you okay? Besides totally in shock?" Justin's hand reached blindly for her.

Holly gripped his hand, continually crying. She would be the puffiest-eyed bride ever. "You were a part of this?"

"Well, yeah. It would've been hard to have a wedding without the groom, ya know?"

She laughed. "I mean, you really want to do this?"

"It's all for you, Honey. We said we would have a real wedding one day, when the time was right. I was going to wait until after Tina and Bo got hitched, see how you reacted to theirs. Then Tina and Jayden cornered me, and next thing you know, I'm renting a tux. It's more of a hostage situation for both of us at this point." He chuckled.

"Did Tina use power tools? She has that nasty habit, you know." Holly leaned her head against the door. She caressed his hand. "Your nails are clean, baby. I'm so proud."

"Your effing brother made me get a manicure."

Holly bit her bottom lip to keep from laughing at him. He did not sound thrilled about that.

"I've never felt so feminine in my life," Justin grumbled and Holly lost the battle. "I guess it's worth it, though."

"Aw, baby, that's thoughtful of you." Holly brought his hand to her mouth and kissed his knuckles and then his fingertips.

"Will you remarry me, Holly?"

Holly placed his hand over her heart. "Yes. A thousand times over, yes. I love you so much and I want the world to know. Let's do this."

"I'm glad you said yes. I paid a pretty hefty deposit on this tux, and there's like a million flowers and chairs on the boat dock, so, yeah, that would be awkward otherwise."

She laughed again, knowing he was intentionally trying to be funny to calm her down.

"I love you, Holly Grace Combs. And I'm ready to say that in front of God and everybody." He pulled on her hand and she felt his lips caress her palm.

Hours later, after hair, makeup, and four people helping

her into her dress, Holly and her bridesmaids lined up. Her father came to escort her down the aisle.

"You must love this boy if you're marrying him twice." He winked and kissed her forehead. "I'm glad to be a part of it this time, Honey."

"Daddy, I'm sorry about all of that—"

"Shh." He waved her off. "It's your wedding day. You don't have to apologize for anything, not today."

Hunter came up and stood on the opposite side of her dad. Holly tilted her head and raised her brows.

"What?" He adjusted his tie, not looking at her. "I gave you away once and it didn't stick. I have to make sure he takes you this time." Hunter grinned and wiggled his brows. "You are radiant, sis. A true masterpiece."

Holly's lip trembled as she mouthed *thank you*, unable to speak.

As the music played and the procession began, Holly was overwhelmed with how the backyard and boat dock had been transformed with Christmas lights, flowers, and tulle. The river sparkled in the fading sunlight, adding to the incredible scenery. She held Hunter's hand and looped her hand with her bouquet through her dad's arm. They held her up straight when her knees buckled under the thrill of it all.

Standing by the same preacher who had married them years ago was the most handsome man on God's green earth.

Justin.

Everything else faded away. They locked eyes and he smiled ear-to-ear, his soulful brown eyes full of happiness. Holly's tears were gone, replaced with a matching smile. There he was, her husband and best friend, her childhood sweetheart, her champion who never gave up on them.

Holly couldn't restrain herself. The last few feet of the aisle, she released her father and brother and ran straight into Justin's arms. Their friends laughed and the preacher wiped a tear.

"I'd ask who gives 'er away," said the preacher, "but I reckon she's past that point."

Justin and Holly smiled and laughed, holding hands.

"Hey," Hunter said, extending a hand to Justin. "Hang on to her this time, okay?"

Justin shook his hand. "I will, bro. I will."

As the ceremony started, the preacher teased about having déjà vu. Holly vaguely remembered reciting vows that had been adjusted to fit their situation. The whole ceremony was like a dream. The only thing that she could recall for sure was how Justin kissed the bride and her world spun as cheers erupted.

Tina sang as they danced their first dance officially as husband and wife and Holly's heart danced on cloud nine.

"I love you, Mr. Meyers. Always have, always will."

"I love you too, Mrs. Meyers."

"You're the best man I know, Justin. All these years, your love has run steady, like the river, connecting us, even when I didn't realize it. You give me hope and courage and I know that our marriage is going to be as steadfast as you are." She gave him a kiss that earned them a few whistles. Holly took a deep breath and hoped her timing was right. They were alone on the dance floor, no one else to hear her words. "I'm glad we didn't wait until after Tina and Bo's wedding this Christmas before we did this."

"Why is that?" Justin's hazel eyes glittered with inner joy.

"Because maternity wedding dresses are *so* not my style."

Justin froze. They stood perfectly still on the dance floor as he soaked that in. His jaw flopped open. "Maternity? As in—" Air rushed from his mouth. "Holy shit. You're… you're…"

She nodded. "I'm pregnant. I was going to tell you next week after my doctor's appointment. But—"

Justin picked her up so fast, she screamed. He spun her around, and when he set her down on her feet, he turned around and hollered, "We're pregnant! We're going to have a baby!"

Holly covered her face, mortified that he had told everyone. There she stood in her white wedding dress, knocked up. If that wasn't a redneck cliché, she didn't know what was.

Par for the course with us. The thought made her laugh. Nothing about their relationship made sense or played by the rules. It just…worked.

Cheers erupted and the party took on a whole new life.

Justin held her and his eyes glistened. "You've made me the happiest man alive, Honey. I promise I'll be the best husband and father I can be. You'll never have to doubt my love for you and our family. If nothing else, have faith in that promise."

"I always have, always will." Holly kissed him hard. It took her four years, but she finally got it right.

THE END…FOR NOW.

LYNETTE STRETCHED UNDER THE FINE SILK SHEETS AND languidly rolled over to find Jonathan naked in bed with her. Three months ago, they had met on an elevator in her office building and they became fast friends, and even faster lovers.

Jonathan was in line for a major promotion at his advertising company after landing a huge deal with an up-and-coming video game creator, and Lynette worked for a law firm three floors up from their office. He brazenly invited her to lunch right in the elevator and that lunch turned into dinner, which turned into an incredibly active love affair.

Now, three months later, she watched him sleep and marveled at his stunning good looks, the way his body could manipulate hers in ways she never imagined, and how, when they weren't in bed, they joked and talked about life, debated theology, and shared stories from their various world travels. Jonathan was the best thing about DC.

Being ever so careful, she slid out of bed, grabbed one of his shirts, and padded to the kitchen to make coffee. If she was quiet, she might even pull off surprising him with breakfast. Every little sound woke him up, so she had to be extra sneaky in the mornings.

Coffee was easy enough; she simply pushed the button. Lynette bit her bottom lip and grinned at how good her body felt after last night's acrobatic sex. She danced around the kitchen, singing in her head, and gathered up ingredients for pancakes.

As she passed the hall leading to the front door, she nearly screamed at the woman standing in the doorway.

A tiny tot pointed a finger. "Mommy, ders a neked lady in the kishen."

"How did you get in here?" Lynette pulled at the shirt to make sure her lady regions were covered. "Who are you?"

"I have a key, because this is *my* house. Who the hell are you?" The short, slightly plump woman dropped her bags of groceries and moved aside so that two very young children could come inside.

Nausea hit Lynette as deadly as the knife in her heart.

The children were carbon copies of Jonathan.

"MaryAnne?" From behind Lynette, Jonathan emerged from the bedroom with only a sheet around his waist. "What are you doing here?"

MaryAnne held back the two young children, who reached for their daddy. "I came to surprise my husband for the weekend. But looks like I'm the one with the surprise."

"Honey, we can talk about this—"

Lynette held up her hands. "Hold the fucking phones." She glanced at the children, a little boy and girl, close in age, maybe three and four, and regretted the f-bomb explosion. "Sorry."

MaryAnne ushered them into the formal dining room and closed the doors. She didn't say a word.

Lynette took a deep breath and glared at Jonathan. She kept her voice calm as she asked her questions through gritted teeth. "You're *married*? This is your *wife* and those are your *children*?" Anger brought out the part of her known in court as a she-devil.

"Lynette, baby, I can explain everything."

"Shut up," she snapped, her fierce nature taking over.

MaryAnne must have been in shock, because she simply stared at Jonathan with anguish on her face and tears welling up in her eyes. There would be no anger support coming from her.

"You've been lying to me for three months?"

"Three months?" MaryAnne gasped and threw out her hand to brace herself against the wall. Tears streamed down her face.

Lynette turned to the wife. "You didn't know?"

Brown hair shook wildly on her head. "We live three hours away. We bought this place when he got the job offer so he wouldn't have to commute." MaryAnne raised her eyes to Jonathan. "You said it was work. I haven't seen you in *weeks* because you said you were so busy at the office. How could you?"

Jonathan took a step in their direction, one hand reaching for his wife, the other holding his sheet. "Honey, I'm sorry. I have been working, and I just, I got lonely. And—"

"And nothing, asshole!" Lynette took a protective step in front of MaryAnne and slapped away his hand. "I can't believe you! That's the best reason you can come up with for cheating on your wife and lying to me? You got lonely? Get a fucking dog," she screamed, then realized the kids probably heard it. She turned to MaryAnne and whispered, "Shit, I'm sorry." Some things you couldn't beat out of a southern girl, and as a general rule, you didn't curse in front of the kids.

MaryAnne waved it off and continued to quietly cry. "Least of my worries."

This poor woman. Lynette saw the pain and shock and fear on her face, in the way her eyes moved around with each passing thought in her mind. She rounded on Jonathan and fisted her hands. All this time that he had been seducing her, making love to her, talking about life and their future, he was lying. As much as her heart broke, it was MaryAnne that she truly felt hurt for. It was his two little children who had this douchebag as a father that caused her anger to rise. "Let's find out fact versus fiction?"

Jonathan recognized the wildness rise to the surface. His eyes widened. "Lynette, don't do anything stupid."

Lynette grabbed a vase from the side table and held it out to his wife. "Family heirloom?"

MaryAnne's brows furrowed. "Garage sale."

"Good." She launched the vase at the wall right beside Jonathan's head.

He screamed and shielded himself from the blow. "Damn it, Lynette! You nearly hit me!"

"That's the point. I meant to hit the wall." She picked up another clay sculpture and showed it to MaryAnne. "Trip to Africa?"

"Trip to a half-rate amusement park safari." MaryAnne wiped her tears. Anger finally registered in the other woman's tone. *Good.*

In high school and her first year of college, Lynette Miller earned many softball scholarships. She still held the record for number of strikeouts in a single season in her home town of Riverview. She could out-pitch any of the boys and *always* hit where she aimed.

"Lynette, don't you do it," Jonathan growled and came at her.

"Wrong approach." She hurled the little elephant statue at him and whizzed by, mere centimeters from his face.

He sneered. "You missed."

"Made you look." Lynette wound up and pitched a marble ball she had grabbed from a decorative bowl.

Jonathan's eyes widened.

The marble ball hit him square in the crotch and he crumpled to the ground in slow motion. His face turned a frightening shade of purple and he moaned in pain.

From behind her, MaryAnne huffed a laugh. She had her mouth covered and her eyes were as big as plates. She met Lynette's eyes and they shared a satisfied smile.

"Get those pretty babies out of here. I'll give you the name of a ruthless divorce lawyer. He hates me, so he'll be more than happy to take this case. I'll give you everything you need to leave Jonathan shirtless."

She proudly stalked off to the bedroom and put on her pants. She gathered her things, controlled her own tears, and stepped over Jonathan, who still lay in the fetal position in the hallway, moaning and cross-eyed.

He reached for her ankle. "You can't do this. I love you both." He could barely whisper the words between his groans.

"Love?" she huffed and crouched down in his face. "You don't know the meaning of the word. The only thing you love is yourself. If you knew what love was, you would've been loyal to your *wife*, honest with me, and set a better example for those two children. You don't know love. You don't deserve love, not mine, and damn sure not hers." She pointed to MaryAnne, who waited in the doorway. "We all deserve better than you." She rose with the shredded remains of her dignity and marched out of the house and into the street.

People in the neighboring townhouses were up and sitting on their stoops, drinking their morning coffee and watering what tiny little yards they had in this part of Washington, DC.

"You know, I don't think you're the first." MaryAnne shivered and hugged herself. "There was this girl in his office back home. She was a nobody, a tramp trying to sleep her way to the top. She worked as his PA for a while, even bought me flowers on my birthday." She rubbed her temple and rolled her eyes. "I'm a fool. A complete fool. I put my dreams on hold so I could take care of our kids and be a good wife, so that he could pursue his career."

Lynette put a hand on her elbow. "Don't you make this a pity party. He's a lying sack of shit. You and your kids deserve better." She dug out a card from her purse and scribbled a phone number on it. "You call that lawyer and you make sure that you get back everything you've sacrificed for him tenfold. Do *not* be the weepy wife…unless you're in court…then you milk that cow for all it's worth. Those kids need you to be strong and take care of business, got it?"

MaryAnne nodded. "You know, at least with you, I get it. I never did understand the floozy at his office, but you…" She wiped the tears from her face. "Well, I get it."

Lynette bit the inside of her cheek to keep from crying. She couldn't very well tell this woman to stay strong if she was on the verge of a mental breakdown. "For what it's worth, I am so sorry. I didn't know. And if I did—"

"You would've pegged him in the balls sooner?"

"Twice." Lynette covered her sadness with sarcasm. "Once for me and once for you." She turned her face away. "Call that guy. Today."

"What are you going to do?" Her concern touched Lynette.

Life in DC had not been what she expected in the months she had been here. She wasn't too fond of her job, or her boss, or the multiple blocks she had to hike to work every day. With the illusion of a fantasy relationship with Jonathan blown to hell, there wasn't too much of DC she cared to stick around for.

Tina Foster, one her best friends since childhood, was only a few months away from getting married. Lynette hadn't intended to go to the wedding because of work… and because she had tried so hard to outgrow the little town lifestyle.

After the last hour, Riverview didn't look so bad. "I think I might go home."

She smiled at MaryAnne and headed down the sidewalk.

When she was safely tucked away in her matchbox apartment, she curled up on her bed and let the tears flow until her eyes were swollen and she cried herself to sleep.

Four months, and one horrible divorce case later, her name was splashed all over the local news as the "home-wrecker with heart." Lynette had been true to her word and helped MaryAnne get everything she could from Jonathan. In return, MaryAnne gifted her a BMW, a present from MaryAnne's father to Jonathan in celebration of his big new job in the city.

It turned out that MaryAnne's family was incredibly wealthy, which was why Jonathan couldn't stand to lose her.

His car, his apartment, and his fancy clothing were all from the generosity of his in-laws.

Lynette was happy to know that the mother and children wouldn't be left out in the cold; far from it. Her lawyer frenemy tried to keep her name out of the news as professional courtesy, but the story was too good for Jonathan's lawyer to keep quiet.

Lynette read the headline in the paper. "A Home-Wrecker with Heart: how one lawyer sabotaged a marriage but saved a family." The headline that got her fired.

She tossed the newspaper out of the window of her brand new BMW and watched in the rearview as the sheets scattered in the wind, Washington, DC disappearing in the background.

Riverview, Texas was a long drive from DC, which meant she had plenty of time to think about what she was going to say to her parents. "Sorry I haven't called in a few years" was at the top of her list.

The road home was beautiful and would help clear her mind. Her mother always told her, "If you get lost in this big world, just follow the river home." That was exactly what she was going to do.

Dialing the number of the only person she knew would understand, she took a deep breath. "Hello, gorgeous."

Gasp. "Lynette, is that you? Please tell me I'm not dreaming and this is actually my favorite cousin on the line."

"It's me, Jayden. I need a place to stay for a while."

"You're coming home? Thank fu—"

To be continued…

Sample of Book One

why the River Runs

Bo's foot tapped the floor as he waited for Mr. Foster to read over his resume. The writing on the paper was sparse, seeing how there wasn't much to report for the last four years. This job meant a lot. It was a fresh start, a new beginning, a clean slate. Coming home to Riverview and working at Foster's represented all these things and more. Foster Construction could be his ticket to redemption.

Okay, maybe that was putting too much pressure on one interview. But it would be ideal if he could get in with one of the biggest companies in the county. Especially since his grandmother knew someone who knew someone who was friends with Duane Foster and they might skip the background check based on the recommendation.

"You've done construction?" Duane's thick gray brows rose as he read the resume over the top of his readers.

"Y'sir," Bo answered. Even years in California couldn't beat his country accent out of him.

"Carpentry, huh?"

"Y'sir."

"Where did you learn?"

Jail. "On-the-job experience."

"With who?"

"The State."

"And who can I contact as a reference over there?"

Bo paused. *My parole officer?* Sweat dripped down the back of his neck. He wasn't prepared for the stare-down. Even the Border Collie sitting beside the desk gawked.

Duane let out a long breath and swiped a hand down his face. He leaned over his beat-up metal desk and braced himself on his elbows. "All right, son, let's cut the bull, shall we?"

Dang it. Here it came. The *I'm sorry we don't hire criminals* speech. It would be the third one he'd received since he got out. Bo looked down at his work boots. His grandmother had bought them brand new just for this interview. She lived on social security and selling produce from her own garden, but she'd spent all her extra money that month for the steel-toed boots. All he wanted to do was pay her back with a little good news.

"I talked to your grandmother already, Bo." There was a hint of affection in his voice. "Sweet lady, right there."

He nodded and glanced at his boots. "Y' sir." As hard as it was, he kept his chin up.

Duane steepled his fingers. "Said you just got out. How long you been home, son?"

"Two weeks, sir."

Duane nodded. "Welcome back to civilization. Have a

probation officer?"

"Parole, sir. Got out three years early. Have to check in monthly and prove I'm working, sir."

"She said you did four years. What for?"

Shit. Bo met Duane's gaze. He'd paid his time for a crime he wasn't too terribly sorry for. "Found my step-dad hitting my mother. I returned the gesture. Judge decided since I was a black belt, and I didn't exactly hold my punches, it qualified as assault with a deadly weapon. That's a felony in California."

Duane nodded his head and pursed his lips. "What brings you to Texas?"

"A promise I made to my grandmother and a fresh start."

Duane leaned in, narrowing his gaze. "Do you consider yourself a violent man, Bo?"

How many times had people asked him that question? At least half a dozen. The parole board, his anger management counselor, the judge. This was the first time he looked the person across the table square in the eyes and answered bluntly. "Only when a woman is confused with a punching bag, sir."

"Can't blame you there." Duane's astute eyes narrowed as he leaned back and rested his chin in his hand. He pursed his lips again, studying Bo like he might sprout horns. The dog barked when a door opened and closed down the hall, making Bo flinch. "You have to meet my foreman. Then we'll see."

"Be happy to, sir." Hope lit in his chest. As far as men went, Bo considered himself friendly enough and he knew how to work hard.

Duane's lips stretched into a grin and he huffed. He

lifted his chin and hollered, "T, come here. Got some fresh blood for ya."

Bo stood up to greet the other man, uncomfortable with someone approaching the office door from behind him. He turned and locked his gaze with a pair of blue eyes so light and airy, they stole the breath from his lungs.

"Bo, meet my foreman…Tina."

Tina was a good six inches shorter than his six-foot frame, but her presence loudly stated that she had the upper hand. Sun-streaked blonde hair was pulled back into a haphazard bun with strands escaping. The whole twisted mess was held together with a pencil and a band. He had the sudden—and stupid—urge to pluck it from her hair and watch the mass fall. She wore no makeup, but her thick, black lashes almost looked painted on. From many days in the sun, her skin was a golden brown. The great tan was accentuated by the dirty white tank top. Even her brown carpenter pants were stained at the knees and had sawdust on them. Unlike his, her boots were scuffed and marred, painted with a dozen different colors and substances.

Bo couldn't help himself; he studied her head to toe… twice. This was a woman who knew a hard day's labor. She was also the most angelic woman he'd ever seen. Her high cheekbones and heart-shaped face were dusted with bronze, and thin but tempting lips pursed as she looked him up and down.

Bo stirred, his blood heating, his body instantly reacting to her attention.

After an awkward moment of him standing there with his jaw on the floor, Tina held out her hand. "Tina Foster. Who are you?" Her gaze darted from Bo to Duane and back.

It took him a moment to remember anything but how beautiful she was. *Shit.* "Uh, I, um, I'm Bo Galloway. Nice to meet you, ma'am."

"Likewise. Daddy, we need to deal with a certain painter that's about to burn my biscuits."

Daddy? Of course, this was Duane's daughter. *Double shit.*

"Great," Duane huffed. "Fill me in later."

"You know I will." Tina crouched and rubbed the dog's head, allowing it to lick her cheek. "There's my Dixie girl."

Duane cleared his throat. "Mr. Galloway is Nancy Brewer's grandson. He's returning after far too many years in California."

"The lady who sells the produce, right?" Tina deferred to Duane, who nodded. "Yeah, I thought you looked familiar." She ran her eyes over him once again, her poker face in perfect form. "I didn't realize we were hiring, Dad." She tilted her head at her father.

"We can always use a good hand, you know that."

Tina's lips curled downward. "Everything look tight on paper?"

Duane's eyes met Bo's. For a moment, Bo's heart stopped and he held his breath. One word from Duane and this beautiful, hardworking woman wouldn't give him the time of day—much less a job. Bo pleaded internally. He needed this break.

Duane slid the resume into his desk drawer and glanced at a spot on the wall. "Yup. Looks good on the paperwork end."

Thank God.

"Now you can see if he's worth a darn in the field."

"All right." Tina nodded once, put her hands on her

hips, and scowled at him, giving the same contemplating look as her father. "Two things before I let you on my job site."

"Here we go," Duane muttered, turning his attention back to his laptop.

Tina held up one finger. "First off, if you've got issues taking orders from someone with a vagina," she pointed said finger to the door of the office, "there's the door. Don't waste my time. I don't have patience for chauvinistic BS. Two, if you don't like country music, I suggest you invest in noise-canceling ear plugs. You'll work on my site until I see what you can do, then you might be transferred to one of our other crews. When can you start?"

"How fast can you write the address?" Bo said.

"Slow down, son. We have to fill out paperwork." Duane laughed and waved Bo to come sit back down.

Maybe there was a God after all. If so, He was smiling down on Bo at that moment. Bo called his grandmother to tell her he would be busy at lunch.

❦

The country music comment was understood immediately. Bo parked his late grandfather's rusted Ford on the construction site and exited the truck to the local country music station blaring from a radio. He traded his button-down for a company tee-shirt and searched for Tina.

"You the new guy?" A tall man with salt and pepper hair and matching beard gave him a speculative glance. "Duane called me a minute ago."

Bo swallowed and looked upwards. "Yes, sir."

He thrust out a hand. "Great. T's upstairs. She's hanging the sheetrock in the bedrooms. Take this." Terry handed him a box of screws. "I'm gonna get the next boards ready."

Bo nodded, accepting the screws.

"I'm Terry Hicks, her right-hand man. Word of advice: don't argue with her and don't hit on her. You're likely to get your nuts shot off with a nail gun either way."

Instinctually, Bo covered himself, cringing. What the hell did he just walk into? "You give that speech often?"

Terry grinned, his age apparent in every wrinkle on his face. "Every chance I get. I'm her uncle."

Bo nodded and headed inside the gutted two-story ranch house, stepping over tools and wires. Each room was in various stages of renovation. He found Tina and two other guys in an upstairs bedroom.

"Crapballs." Tina let out a guttural growl as she snapped the battery back on her cordless drill. "These things don't last more than five freaking minutes." Tina glanced up and back down once she saw him. "Where's Terry?"

"Down there." Bo held out the box of screws. He didn't know what to think of Tina yet. She walked a thin line between being a total bitch or a total badass. Based on the way she gave him the cold shoulder, he was leaning towards the former.

"You know how to hang?" She didn't meet his eyes as she opened the box of screws and poured them into the pocket of her utility belt.

Bo swallowed hard. His experience working construction in high school only lasted a short while. "A little."

Tina sighed and squinted her eyes at the floor. The two seconds she hesitated felt like two hours. "No time like the present." She checked her watch. "Clocking in at ten twenty. Jason, Bill, this is Bo. Let's teach him how to hang wall, m'kay?"

The two other men nodded and smiled. Not overly friendly but not indifferent either. Tina turned her back to him and finished up the piece of drywall she was working on. Bill was older, at least in his forties, and had thinning hair and a pot belly. Jason looked closer to Bo's age, mid-twenties, and wore his baseball cap backwards. He had tats on his forearms and the back of his neck. He at least gave Bo a cordial fist bump.

Bo observed them place a few boards and became momentarily stunned at the quickness with which Tina worked. It took her spare minutes to screw the whole thing to the studs. Terry came in with her next piece. She situated it on the wall and Bo jumped in to hold it steady so she could anchor it.

She crouched down, giving him a great view of her back and ass. "Damn it, Terry. Get your glasses out, old man." Tina examined where the electrical outlet cut out *should've* been.

"What?" he said, bending over to look. "Aw, hell."

"If you don't start wearing your glasses on the job, I'm going to staple them to your stubborn head." Tina straightened.

"I got it." This was one thing he could do. Bo grabbed the measuring tape from her belt and measured for the outlet, using Terry's pencil to mark it on the drywall. He tossed the tape back to Tina and grabbed the mechanical handsaw on the ground behind them all. He made a precise and even cut, perfectly framing the blue outlet casing.

"Thanks." Tina pointed a finger at him. "But don't touch my belt again."

"Yes, ma'am."

Terry shook his head and laughed. "I'll get him a tool belt. We don't need another lawsuit." He went back downstairs.

"*Another* one?" Bo stared off after Terry. Jason chuckled, Bill shivered.

Tina merely shrugged and rolled her eyes, returning to her task like it was no big deal. What the hell kind of woman was he dealing with? Lawsuits over tools, nailing testicles, stapling glasses to heads. Dear God. He definitely wasn't in California anymore.

Damn, it was nice to be back in the South. He'd almost forgotten what country girls were like.

For the rest of the morning, he trod carefully around Tina Foster. She had no problems telling him exactly what she wanted him to do and how she wanted it done. Every move she made was calculated and skillful. The woman was all business, except for when certain songs came on the radio. Then the whole crew tried to out sing one another. The only time she stopped working was when she danced over to pick up a tool or twirled around in place to the beat.

The crazy thing was, the chick had a good set of pipes on her. She kept up with the radio singers without breaking her working stride. The guys on the crew couldn't carry a tune in a five-gallon bucket, but that didn't stop them from loudly following along, creating a painful racket.

If there was one thing Bo learned by working construction years ago, it was that men would relate everything to their penises. Everything could be turned into a sexual innuendo, and filters worked best on machinery, not mouths. Cussing was not only standard conversation, it was practically a requirement of the job.

He wondered how having Tina in the mix affected that

atmosphere. Throwing a woman in the ring didn't faze them a bit. Hell, Tina didn't hold her tongue either. She gave those guys a hard time every chance she was given. They teased, laughed, cursed, and pranked each other like…well, like one big happy family. Everyone knew their places, knew their roles, and did their jobs efficiently.

He could only hope to carve out a place for himself in this well-oiled machine of a crew.

At the end of the day, Bo was tired and completely satisfied. Just before they'd called it quits, Tina walked him to his truck.

"Not bad, Galloway. See you back here tomorrow at six."

"Six?" He leaned his head in as if he didn't hear her. On the job at six in the morning, he could handle that. He was used to breakfast call at 5:30.

"The earlier we get started, the earlier we can call it a day. Summer in Texas is brutal, Galloway. It's no fun working in the afternoon heat. Get to bed early, bring lots of water." She spun on her heel and gave him a view of her round backside. He nearly dropped his keys.

As she walked away, a song came to his mind. To see her smile, he'd do anything. He didn't care for country music, but if it meant being around Tina Foster all day, he'd learn to love it.

⁂

That evening, he pulled up to his grandmother's old farmhouse. Besides the flowers, it hadn't changed since he was a child. The same swing hung on the porch, the screen door still had a hole in it from when his mother kicked it. The paint needed refreshing and the gravel driveway was losing the war with the grass, but the house had never looked better to him.

For three weeks, since his grandmother had driven all the way to southern California to pick him up, she had sat at the dinner table and prayed every night that he would find a job. Tonight, he had good news for her.

Nan came out the front door, her arms up in the air in triumph, a huge smile on her face.

Bo's face matched hers as he climbed the stairs and hugged her.

"See, I told you praying helps. I'm so proud, Bo."

"Thanks, Nan. Now all I have to do is keep it."

She waved a bony arm, dismissing his pessimism. "Nonsense. You're going to excel, I just know it."

Bo held open the door for her.

"You've never been lazy, Bo Allen. You just put that determination of yours to good use and the Fosters are going to be sending me a fruit basket. Just wait and see."

He treasured the confidence she had in him. When it felt like all the world had abandoned him, Nan had stood like a lighthouse in the storm. He had promised his grandfather he would take care of her and he would make good on it.

"I made your favorite, chicken fried steak. There's sweet tea in the fridge and," she bent to pull a cake out of the oven, "I made you a pineapple cream cake." Her face glowed, truly glowed, with happiness for him.

"Dang, Nan. I need to get a job every day."

"Son, we are going to celebrate every little victory we can." She kissed his cheek and immediately spit like she'd licked a lemon. "Ugh, you're dirty. I think I just ate sawdust. Go get cleaned up, working man."

Bo laughed. "Yes, ma'am." If he gave her a million dollars a day for the rest of his life, it would never be enough to repay her for everything she'd given him. Maybe he could start by working on her house.

<hr>

Tina fell into her father's office chair with a cloud of dust rising into the air. She was tired to the bones, a good feeling. It hurt to rub Dixie's head, but she couldn't withhold love from her favorite girl.

"How'd he do?" Daddy shut his laptop.

She didn't require an explanation of who he was talking about. "Fine. Didn't say ten words all day and probably thought we're all bat-shit crazy."

Her father chuckled, knowing all too well about their singing rituals and Tina's habitual dancing while she worked.

"That's to be expected. Think he'll stick?"

She shrugged and dusted off her shirt. "Hell if I know. He's awful quiet to fit in around here. What's his deal? We weren't looking to hire anyone."

Daddy shifted in his chair. "It's a favor for an old friend."

Picking up on her father's reluctance to broach the subject, she leaned over and pinned him with her stare. "What's his deal, Dad? I know something's off."

"How can you tell?"

"His boots. You and I know the only time a person in construction has new boots is around Christmas and their birthday. So, unless he blew out some candles recently, he hasn't seen work in a while."

Daddy nodded, the corner of his mouth pulled back into a smirk. "He's had a rough go at it, T. Give him a chance. He needs the work."

Tina tilted her head and nodded. Her father had a soft heart, but she was trying to run a business, not a shelter for the lost and needy. If Bo Galloway didn't pull his weight, he'd be gone. "Dad, I love your heart. But I'm a week behind as it is, and as much as I know you love to take in strays—"

"Dixie was a stray and look how she turned out." Daddy cocked his head to the side.

Tina nodded. Fair point. "What'cha want for dinner?" Joints and muscles complained as she got to her feet.

"It's my turn to cook."

"No arguments here. I hate drywall days. They kill me." She rubbed the base of her back.

Daddy pushed himself out of his chair and grabbed the two canes he required to walk out of the office. If he only needed the canes, then today was a good day. Bad days required the wheelchair. Daddy had broken his back on a job site just after her high school graduation. The surgery to fix his back was a botched job that left him with permanent spinal damage and the inability to walk for more than a few minutes at a time. That was when he and his daughter traded places. Tina had helped in the office. Now, Daddy held the desk job and Tina busted her ass every day.

She wouldn't have it any other way. At least he was alive. The same couldn't be said of her mother, who had died giving birth to her.

They made their way to the back of the building where they lived. The two-story warehouse, formally a cannery, was part of Riverview's history. They loved being able to take care of the building. They'd bought it at auction and renovated every inch of it themselves. Now it stood proudly on the bank of the river as a tribute to the town's history.

Behind the front offices was a one-bedroom apartment for Daddy. Tina lived upstairs in another apartment. She usually ate with her father, caught a game or two, then headed up to her own space.

"You got plans for the weekend?" her father asked over dinner.

Tina was showered and comfy in her sweats, her hair wet around her shoulders. She shook her head and shrugged a shoulder, knowing what her father was really asking. Did she have a date?

Daddy huffed. "That engineer fellow hasn't called you yet?"

Tina blew it off. "Only five or six times…today."

Daddy speared his pasta and put it in his mouth. "I think he's really smitten with you."

"Smitten?" Tina curled her lip up and rolled her eyes. "Daddy, really. Trey is great, but I don't think I want a guy who is *smitten*. Sounds a little soft, you know?"

Not that she would confess that to her father, but soft was exactly how she and her crew described Trey. He was a pencil-pushing, number-crunching, civil engineer who would happily place himself at her heel like a dog. The attention was flattering, she had to admit. Trey doted on her, praised her with gifts and adoration. She would never have to worry about him cheating or running around on her, which he was capable of doing. He had just enough Asian descent to give him the tear-shaped brown eyes and dark features. As her crew said, Trey was pretty. Tina wouldn't disagree. She'd looked at him plenty in the beginning.

"Don't discount him just because he's not as tough as you are. Not many men are." He mumbled the last part as if he didn't want her to hear it. His eyes said it all. Daddy carried a healthy respect for her above and beyond what fathers and daughters share. They were business partners and friends.

"Why don't you plan something with the girls? Keri or Jayden—"

"Dad," Tina cut him off, "why are you so interested in my social life?" Her knee bounced under the table.

He shrugged his wide shoulders. "Aw, I don't know, baby girl. I guess I saw the way Bo looked at you and I realized how often I overlook the fact that you're a pretty young woman who should be fighting men off with a stick." His blue eyes, just like hers, saw far too much these days.

"I do fight men off with a stick, every day. It's usually because they want to wring my neck, but it counts." Tina grinned, hoping to lighten her father's mood. He rolled his eyes. "Daddy, look." She set down her fork and made sure she had his attention. "Right now, Trey and I are just a casual thing. I don't have time for an all-in relationship and he knows that. He says he's okay with it. Jayden is a freaking mess. We're coming up on the anniversary of Chris's death and Keri and I are arguing over how to handle it."

"What do you mean?" Daddy put his elbows on the table and stared at her.

She pulled her hair back and twisted it, playing with the strands, and settled in for a discussion with her father. "Well, I think we need to usher her out of town, take her mind off it. Keri thinks we need to do some sort of balloon release thing. We agreed to take the weekend and think about it, talk to Bear, talk to Chris's mom, and see what the family thinks. I don't know what the answer is. What did you do after Mom died?"

Daddy pursed his lips and squinted his eyes. "It was a

little different. I had you, and you kept me busy. When your mom's birthday came along, you were learning to sit up, so I tried to concentrate on that. The anniversary of her death was your birthday, so we celebrated your birth and her home-going. Jayden doesn't have a baby to keep her mind occupied." He looked down at his plate and his face slipped into sadness. "I guess in some ways, I was lucky to have a piece of your mother left to get me through. All Jayden has is that unfinished house."

"Maybe that's why I don't want to date anyone right now. It's too hard to think about losing them. Besides, I don't need a man. I'm just too busy." Seeing her father's loss and living through Jayden's pain only helped mortar up the cracks that Bo created in her defenses. If she was to save herself the heartache losing the one she loved, it was best not to go down that path at all. Keeping people at arm's length was the simplest solution.

"I know that. You've been independent from your first breath. I know you don't *need* a man, T. I'm just worried that you don't *want* one." Her father sighed, a troubling scowl forming on his face.

"Well, if it makes you feel better, I don't want a girl either." Tina picked up her plate to take it to the sink as her father chuckled, put his hands together in prayer, and mouthed *thank you Lord* to the ceiling.

Tina thumped him in the back of the head as she walked past and he laughed. "What? I want grandbabies."

"You find a man who can keep up with me, Daddy, and we'll talk." She kissed his head as she came back to pick up his dishes. "I have our company to run and that's my priority."

Daddy gently touched her arm. "Loneliness is a sneaky

demon, Tina Marie. You work so hard you don't realize it's sitting in the same room with you until it's too late."

"You should practice what you preach, old man." Tina winked at him. As much as she joked about it, she was as worried about her father being alone as much as he was worried about her. Neither of them had a thriving social life, but they had friends. Being single in a small town presented challenges people from the city didn't understand. If you weren't related to half the town, then you grew up with them and already knew them far too well to ever consider dating them.

The only reason Trey was in the picture was because he was the engineer on a job they had done in another town. The clients wanted a tornado shelter dug into their foundation in the garage and Tina contacted his agency. It was all good at first, but they were both so involved with their jobs that an actual relationship was too much trouble. Trey was cute and scratched an itch, but that was about it.

Once the kitchen was clean and her father was properly settled back with a beer and his remote, she retreated upstairs. Her apartment was the entire second floor of the warehouse. Brick walls and support columns, fifteen-foot ceilings, old wood floors complete with all the scars and marks from the cannery, large arched windows, and thirty-five hundred square feet of space all hers. She loved the industrial feel, the way the ducts and pipes ran along the ceiling, the way the length of the building faced the river, affording her one of the best views in town.

Tina fixed herself a glass of iced tea and went out to the balcony to watch the boats go by.

I saw the way Bo looked at you today...

Yeah, she'd caught that too. He'd wavered all day

between fear and awe. More than once, she'd caught him staring as if he couldn't tear his eyes away from her. Bo would blink, blush, and turn elsewhere.

The problem was, she was just as dumbstruck by him. Bo Galloway was flaming, smoking, fan-yourself-and-clench-your-thighs hot. He was at least six feet of toned muscle, tattoos, and deeply soulful hazel eyes. Prying her attention from his full bottom lip was harder than she thought possible. Usually, she liked her men to have longer hair, but his dark brown buzz cut fit him just fine. So did his slightly shadowed jaw.

It was all she could do to act normal. The truth was, her sweat hadn't been just from the work site. He'd worn cologne to the interview and she could smell it as he heated up throughout the day. It tickled her senses, made her dizzy. Not to mention that quiet, respectful tone of voice he used with her. The rich, husky texture slid over her like a caress, lighting her up in dark places.

He was brand new to her work crew and yet today he'd been a valuable set of hands. If everything worked out with him, he might help them finish this house under budget. It was a lot cheaper hiring one man for two weeks than to have her entire crew out there for a couple extra days.

Too bad he was such a sexy distraction. Twice she'd lost her train of thought and had to go back inside to re-measure for a cut. One look at Bo lifting dry wall over his head, flexing his bulging arm muscles, stretching out his defined back, and she was like a drooling teenager.

She didn't need this right now. Or ever. Men like Bo didn't stick around and she was dealing with a disastrous dating life as it was. Somewhere along the way, her brain had begun to function more like all the men she was surrounded by. She had a one-track mind; single in focus and hard to derail. She'd given up trying to be overly feminine with makeup and an actual hairstyle, at least from Monday to Friday.

Even her current love interest was more high maintenance than she was. Trey was fond of his expensive suits and his office job. He drove a nice car, styled his dark hair, and his face could stop traffic…except for when it came to her. There was something about him that she couldn't name. Something that made her keep him at arm's length, even though they'd been together for months.

The bigger problem was, as she drifted to sleep, it wasn't Trey on her mind. It was Bo.

Why the River Runs is available now!

About The Author

JoAnna Grace lives in a world of alpha males and strong females where true love conquers all—at least in her books! A proud indie, she has published over ten novels including The Divine Chronicles, the Blake Pride Series, and more. This writer loves to read contemporary, paranormal, and urban fantasy romance novels. She also loves to see new writers take their first steps into being authors, which is how Y&R Publishing came to life.

From the time she started holding a crayon she began to create magical worlds. Living in the real world was never an option. JoAnna's tales are spun at her home in East Texas where she lives with her Prince Charming, three kids, and a couple dogs and cats. When not hiding behind the computer screen chugging coffee, you can find her having fun with her family, singing, or managing multiple businesses.

Share a link to this book on social media!

Tag Jo and share this book with your friends.

Facebook: facebook.com/joannagraceauthor
Twitter: twitter.com/joannagrace4ya
Instagram: instagram.com/authorjoannagrace

Make sure you're in the know. Sign up for the newsletter today!

Do you want to help an author? **Leave a review!** Your opinion matters. Every review can help.

JOANNA GRACE
Giving Wings to Words

www.ingramcontent.com/pod-product-compliance
Lightning Source LLC
Chambersburg PA
CBHW030639190726
48286CB00008B/2581